THREE TERRIFYING TALES OF TERROR!

TALES of Terror

PREPARE TO BE SCARED

TONY BRADMAN

THREE TERRIFYING TALES OF TERROR!

ILLUSTRATED BY

Martin Chatterton

EGMONT

TONY BRADMAN - WORDS

I WAS BORN IN LONDON IN 1954, and was terrified at an early age by a lizard that fell out of a tree that I mistook for a deadly snake; my grandmother, who took snuff and threatened me with a cane when I was naughty; and possible gory death when I ran through the window of a launderette, shattering the glass into tiny pieces with my head. These days I try to avoid things like that, and get most of my frights from watching scary movies and reading scary books. Or writing them.

I still live in London, a dark and ancient city, full of odd corners where nasty things have happened, and where I sometimes worry about bumping into my grandmother's ghost. It hasn't happened yet, but if it does, I might just turn the experience into another 'Tale of Terror'. I hope reading this one scares you as much as writing it terrified me . . .

MARTIN CHATTERTON - PICTURES

IT WAS ALL GOING SO WELL UNTIL Bradman came along ... An idyllic upbringing in Liverpool. College. Marriage to a devoted wife. Two lovely children. A faithful dog. Twenty years spent quietly illustrating, designing and writing all over the world. I had a good life. A secure, unremarkable, safe existence. And then ... then ... Bradman made me work on 'Tales of Terror' and everything changed.

I haven't slept in weeks. I daren't - the nightmares will come back. The voices keep asking me to come out but I won't; not yet. They can't make me. I'm safe in here. Safe with the lights on and the door locked and bolted ...

Let me give you a word of advice. Come closer. I don't want them to hear. Right up to the crack in the door. I'll whisper it. 'Don't read this book!'

EGMONT

We bring stories to life

First published in Great Britain 2004
This edition published 2005
by Egmont UK Limited
239 Kensington High Street, London W8 6SA

Text copyright © 2004 Tony Bradman
Illustrations copyright © 2004 Martin Chatterton

The moral rights of the author and illustrator has been asserted

ISBN 1 4052 2312 X

1 3 5 7 9 10 8 6 4 2

A CIP catalogue record for this title is available
from the British Library

Printed and bound in Great Britain by the CPI Group

CONTENTS

FINAL CUT

CONTENTS

IN HIDING

It's the end of the school day, and Billy Gibson is hiding in the boys' toilets.

Billy stands in a closed cubicle, his back to the door, his bag clutched to his chest. He listens as the building beyond empties.

Above him, grey winter light seeps in from the line of narrow windows over the sinks, but the cold air is already thickening into late afternoon darkness. Billy shifts his feet uneasily. His mouth is dry and he can feel his heart thudding in his chest.

He wonders if it's safe yet to go outside, make a dash for home.

The school slowly grows quieter, the shouts and screams fading to distant murmurs, the thuds of heavily shod feet in the corridors becoming the tap-tapping of a single pair of shoes, silence falling at last. Billy holds his breath, waits a few more seconds . . . and the silence continues unbroken. Time to get moving, he thinks, breathing out, hitching his bag on to his shoulder.

He slips from the cubicle, heads for the door into the corridor, his own footsteps echoing in the room. He reaches for the door-handle – but the door swings open before his hand touches it and three boys stride in.

The one in the middle is fair-haired and much the same size as Billy. He has a small, narrow mouth and pointed features. The other two are big and solidly built, both with their heads shaved close to the skull, the pair almost indistinguishable from each other. Billy knows who all three of them are, and he breathes in sharply. He retreats as they advance, and soon finds himself backed up against the sinks. He covers his chest with his bag, his heart whacking wildly against his ribs now. Like a caged bird trying to escape, Billy thinks, part of his mind oddly distant, observing.

He feels sick, his stomach twisting into a knot.

'Well, here's where you are, Billy,' says the fair-haired boy, coming to a halt in front of him. 'We've been looking for you everywhere, haven't we, lads?' The other two don't answer, take up positions on either side of Billy. 'I was beginning to think you might be hiding from us,' continues the fair-haired boy, smiling at him. 'Although why would you want to do that?'

Because you're Mickey Travis, the school's top hardnut, thinks Billy, and Tweedledum and Tweedledee here are your thugs, and the three of you have been bullying me for the past month. But the thought remains unvoiced.

The bullying had started when Billy had got a good mark for some English homework – a story he'd written, and the teacher had told the class. There had been a little light pushing and shoving afterwards, but Billy had ignored it, hoping that if he didn't make trouble, Mickey would lose interest and move on to somebody else. The rough stuff got heavier, though, Mickey and his lads adding slaps and kicks to another bout of jostling the next day.

Billy put up with that too, choosing to take the line of least resistance, worried that if he didn't he'd only make Mickey angry and things would get worse. Which they did anyway, Mickey graduating to demanding money with his menaces, the slaps becoming punches, the kicks a lot more painful.

So Billy had decided it was time to devise a new plan.

He'd thought about telling his teachers or his mum and dad, but quickly ruled out both options. They probably wouldn't believe him or do anything. And Billy dreaded to think what Mickey might do if he discovered he'd been grassed up. No, Billy had come to the conclusion there was only one thing for it. He would have to keep out of Mickey's way, avoid him. Hide.

But that hasn't worked either, Billy thinks as he stands in the dank gloom of the boys' toilets. Mickey had probably known where he was all the time.

'Hiding? Me?' says Billy nervously. 'What makes you think that?'

'Oh, I don't know,' says Mickey, his smile vanishing. 'I wondered if you might be trying to get out of handing over the money you owe me.'

'Listen, Mickey,' Billy murmurs. 'Can we talk about this?'

'I don't think so, Billy,' says Mickey. 'Do your stuff, boys.'

Mickey steps out of the way, and Billy feels his arms being grabbed, a meaty hand on his neck, his legs kicked from underneath him. Then he's on the floor, his face pushed into the damp, gritty concrete, his nostrils filled with a smell that makes him want to retch, a mixture of old dust and dirt laced with something acrid and foul. He wriggles, tries to get free, but he's held down, Mickey's boys grinding their knees into his back and legs.

He feels Mickey's unhurried, careful hands going through his pockets one by one. And Billy feels other things too: a brief flash of anger at those probing, alien fingers; a sharp, sudden flare of hatred for

Mickey Travis and his lads.

Mickey eventually finds what he's after, takes his fingers away. 'Let him up,' he says, and the other two obey.

Billy rises and brushes the dirt off his clothes, checks himself for any major damage. He seems to be mostly all right, although his cheek is hurting where it was pressed into the floor. Mickey is counting the small collection of coins he's extracted from Billy's pockets. He looks at Billy, frowns.

'Tut, tut, Billy,' Mickey says, and sighs deeply. 'This isn't going to make me rich, is it? You'd better come up with a lot more tomorrow.'

'I . . . I can't,' Billy stammers. 'I mean, I only get my lunch money . . .'

Billy notices that Tweedledum has picked up his bag.

'Well, that's not my problem, is it, Billy?' says Mickey, smiling at him again. 'I'm sure you'll think of something. You're a born loser, pal. It's written all over you, and you'll never, ever change. So we both know you'll always do exactly what I tell you. Just in case, though, here's a sneak preview of what will happen tomorrow – if you let me down.'

Mickey nods at Tweedledum. The boy goes into a cubicle, dumps the contents of Billy's bag into the toilet bowl with a clatter and splash, a red biro glancing off the rim and skittering across the floor to lie at Mickey's feet. He chucks the bag in too, stuffs it in hard, and pulls the chain, grinning.

Mickey picks up the biro, tucks it in Billy's pocket. 'Take my advice, Billy,' he says. 'Be sensible . . . and go with the flow.' His lads smirk, and Mickey laughs softly. 'Believe me, you don't want it to be your head down there next time. So long for now, loser. Enjoy the rest of your day.'

Mickey and his boys make their exit, the door swinging shut behind them, cutting off their loud, echoing laughter. Billy waits for a moment, getting his feelings – and his breathing – under control, trying to calm down. Then he goes into the cubicle to retrieve his bag, salvage his books. But a glance in the bowl tells him he doesn't want to touch either the bag or the books.

He'll have to come up with some excuse, he thinks, say he lost them, left his bag on the bus, take the consequences. He hasn't got any other choice.

Billy opens the door of the boys' toilets. He peers outside, making sure that Mickey and his thugs have really gone. The school's central corridor is reassuringly empty beneath its ceiling lights, pools of brightness alternating with stripes of shadow on the polished floor that stretches ahead of him.

Billy sets off, trudges past dark, deserted classrooms.

He pushes open the doors at the end of the corridor, walks out into the

playground. That's empty as well, black puddles dotted across the tarmac between him and the school's main gates, the sky filling with clouds. He feels the skin tightening over the bones of his face, realises how cold it is. He buttons up his jacket, his breath a silver mist around his head. Billy pauses for a moment. He'll just have to ask his parents for his pocket money early this week. But that's OK, they won't mind. Then he'll be safe, he'll be able to give Mickey more than today. But Billy doesn't feel better, and knows why. He stands brooding, Mickey's words echoing in his mind.

'You're a born loser, pal. It's written all over you . . .'

Billy considers his appearance, wonders

how it's possible to look like a loser and not realise it. He knows he's a bit shy and quiet, not sporty or flash or funny like some people. But there must be something he can shine at, some way of showing Mickey he's not a loser, that there's more to him.

Billy feels the wind whip at his trouser legs, a few spots of rain on his face. It's not a bad plan, he thinks, and starts racking his brains for some activity he could pursue. He's good at writing stories, but that's not going to impress someone like Mickey, is it? Otherwise, Billy's mind is a total blank. He sighs, sets off again, shoulders sagging as he trudges round the school building, following the path to the small back gate he always uses.

The surfaces of the puddles shiver in the

wind, as if an invisible giant has passed a hand across them. Thick clouds shroud the last of the light. Beyond the fence a streetlamp fizzes, then flickers on, and another does the same, then another. Billy's shoes tap-tap on the tarmac. He turns a corner, and suddenly the air before him shimmers for a second. Billy shakes his head . . .

And stops dead in his tracks, his mouth dropping open with surprise.

THE STRANGERS

Billy is facing the part of the playground that's completely hidden from the street, a scruffy patch of cracked tarmac that doglegs round the school and leads to the bike sheds and the small back gate. A rusty fire escape zigzags up the building's four storeys and, at breaktimes, cocky older kids gather in its shadows to pose and smoke when the teachers on duty aren't looking. Other, nastier things have been known to happen there occasionally too.

It should be empty and safe now – but it isn't. It's full of movement and machines and strangers, a bustling crowd of grown-ups under bright lights on stands. Some of them are getting equipment out of a couple of big vans blocking the way to the bike sheds and back gate, others are shouting orders.

Standing at the centre of this mad, chaotic swirl of activity is a tall, slim man in a leather jacket, a huge cigar clamped in his mouth.

Billy sees a large camera being set up beside the man, realises this must be – a film crew! Billy is intrigued, thinks it's so cool, wonders why they're here, assumes they must be using the school as a location. It's odd he hasn't heard anything about it, he thinks. Then he shrugs, decides it's probably being kept quiet to make sure hordes of gawping kids don't hang around.

After all, it isn't every day you get to watch a film crew in action, maybe catch a glimpse of a star or two. That's what Billy wants to do, anyway. He doesn't think anyone has noticed him, and quickly slips into the shadows beneath the fire escape, excited now, determined to see as much as he can. At least it might help him forget his troubles, forget Mickey for a while.

Things gradually settle down as Billy watches, the chaos resolving itself into ordered bustle, then calm, the crew in position. The tall man still stands at the centre of it all, a young woman with a clipboard beside him. The man whispers something to her, and she marches off, heading towards the two vans – and Billy suddenly realises the tall man must be the film's director.

An expectant hush falls, everyone seemingly waiting, the only sounds a soft swish of wind, a discarded sweet wrapper scuffling over the tarmac.

Then a strange, dark figure emerges from one of the vans, a man wearing a top hat and a flowing black cape with a red satin lining. Billy can see he is in make-up, his face a mask of what's supposed to be scarred and burnt flesh. The man is holding a knife, its slender blade flashing under the lights.

Billy knows that the man is an actor, but it's still a spooky sight.

The actor makes his way through the crew, stops in front of them, stands motionless like a wax dummy, the knife by his side. Billy wonders if he's a star, but it could be anybody under that make-up. Billy realises one thing, at least. It must be a horror movie they're shooting here today.

Soon the Clipboard Lady, for that's the name Billy gives her, emerges from the same van, looking rather anxious, hurries back to the Director.

'I'm afraid we might have something of a problem,' she says. 'It seems that no one's actually remembered to book an extra for this scene.'

'What do you mean, no one's remembered?' snarls the Director, turning to glare at her, the cigar moving up and down in the corner of his mouth as he speaks. 'Those damned casting people should have taken care of that!' he continues. 'Now listen, I want you to get on the phone immediately . . .'

'I've spoken to them already,' the Clipboard Lady replies. 'They don't know why it wasn't done, and they can't get an extra at such short notice.'

'Hell's teeth! I don't believe this,' mutters the Director. He takes the cigar from his mouth, drops it to the ground, grinds it under his heel. Billy is fascinated, watches the Director's every move. 'So what am I supposed to do now? The crew's on overtime, I've got a deadline to meet . . .' He paces up and down, stops, glares at the Clipboard Lady again. 'Well, I'm not going to waste a whole night's shooting. We'll have to find an extra ourselves.'

'But I don't see how or where,' says the Clipboard Lady.

Billy notices that most of the crew are no longer taking any notice. Some are reading newspapers, others chatting quietly, and the spooky actor is doing nothing. In fact, he doesn't appear to have moved a single muscle.

Then Billy hears something that almost makes him stop breathing.

'Well, what about . . . him?' says the Director, and points at Billy.

Billy feels time itself stretching, the

Director's gesture somehow slipping into slow motion, his voice deepening, that last word 'him' lengthening, as if it's being pulled from his mouth, his gaze fixed on Billy across the distance between them. And all the others turn now to stare at Billy, their heads moving in unison, their eyes boring into him . . .

BONY FINGERS

Billy panics, retreats further into the shadows, soon finds his back against the wall. He thinks about making a dash for the main gates, but it's too late.

The Director is advancing on him, the

Clipboard Lady in his wake.

Time reverts to its normal speed. Or does it? The Director moves quickly, jerkily almost, his progress marked by sudden leaps during which he appears to cover a lot of ground, like a character in one of those old silent movies. Billy shakes his head, thinks that maybe it's a trick of the lights.

'Hi, there!' says the Director, stopping a couple of metres in front of Billy, at the edge of the fire escape's shadow. He's smiling, but Billy doesn't find that particularly reassuring. 'Now, don't be frightened, I don't bite,' the Director continues. 'Well, not very often anyway,' he adds, and laughs softly. 'So, how would you like to be in the movies, sonny?'

'What, me?' says Billy, his voice embarrassingly squeaky. He can feel himself blushing. 'I wouldn't,' he murmurs. 'Thanks all the same.'

'Come on,' says the Director. 'I'd have thought most kids your age would jump at the chance. Besides, you'll be doing me a real favour.'

'Well . . .' says Billy, and realises the Director has edged closer.

'Great!' the man says, and reaches out to grab Billy's arm.

The power of his grip is disconcerting, his long, bony fingers sinking into the flesh of Billy's right bicep. For an instant Billy hangs back, resisting the pull. Then he gives in, not wanting to cause trouble.

The Director drags Billy off, doesn't let

go till they're standing in front of the crew.
Billy has to shield his eyes from the bright
lights with his hand.

'I'm not sure about this,' the Clipboard
Lady tells the Director.

She's whispering, but Billy can hear her
every word. She must have followed them
over, thinks Billy, although he hadn't
noticed her.

'Quite apart from the insurance
implications,' she says, 'he's obviously got
no experience . . .'

'So what?' the Director snaps. 'If you
ask me, any fool can see he's absolutely
perfect for the job. He certainly won't have
to do any acting . . .'

Billy stands there listening as the two of
them argue, the crew reverting to its

previous state of boredom and inactivity. Billy isn't sure how to take what the Director has just said, but what worries him more is that the Clipboard Lady might manage to talk the Director out of using him.

For Billy has changed his mind. He has decided being in the movies might be a terrific idea, a great opportunity to do something that's way past cool. Billy can imagine the look on Mickey's face when his tormentor discovers that he's in a film. What better way to show Mickey that he isn't a loser?

'Er . . . excuse me?' Billy says, interrupting the argument. The Director and the Clipboard Lady stop talking, turn to look at him. 'I'd really like to do it.'

'Ah, that's the spirit,' says the Director, and grins at him. The Clipboard Lady sighs and rolls her eyes, but the Director ignores her. He puts his arm round Billy, leads him away at speed, Billy feeling as if his feet barely touch the ground till the Director suddenly stops by one of the vans. 'So, you'll probably want to know what you're letting yourself in for, right, sonny?'

'Yes, I would,' says Billy, trying to sound positive and look intelligent, telling himself to go along with what the Director wants, not to spoil things.

'Well, making a movie is rather like making a cake,' says the Director, producing another large cigar and lighting it with lots of puffing. The smoke is thick and white and pungent, a cloud

that soon envelops them both. It catches Billy in the back of the throat and he smothers a cough. 'So what you need first, of course,' the Director says, 'is a good recipe. A script . . .'

Suddenly, under the Director's arm, Billy sees a wodge of paper bound in a red cover, held together by silver split pins. That's very strange, Billy thinks. He doesn't remember seeing the Director holding it before. But he decides that the Director must have had it with him all along and

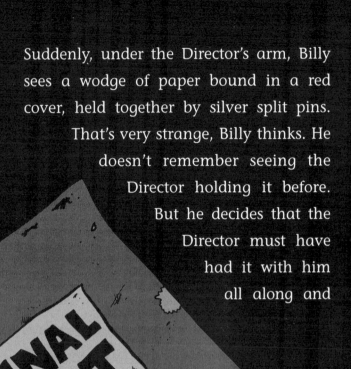

he just hadn't noticed

materialise out of thin a.

at the thought, concen.

Director's voice.

'In a way, the script gives n.   . of
the ingredients that go into the film,' the
Director is saying, 'and instructions on
how to put them together. I also need a few
tools, some utensils.' He pauses, takes the
cigar from his mouth and vaguely gestures
at the crew with it. 'But I'm the one in
charge. I'm the head chef, as it were; I tell
everybody what to do. But even more
important, I'm the one who has "final
cut". Know what that is, sonny?'

'I'm not really sure,' Billy's mind is
filled with an image of the Director cutting
a cake with a knife – like the one the

scary-looking actor is carrying – although he knows that can't be right. From the corner of an eye Billy glimpses some of the crew smirking. But when he glances round, there are no smirks – just blank, expressionless faces staring at him. Billy shivers.

'It means I'm the one who gets to decide what the cake ultimately looks like,' the Director is saying. Billy quickly turns his gaze back to him. 'Once we've done all the actual shooting, I do the editing, I decide which bits of film go where, what gets put in, what gets left out. Control, sonny, that's what matters. Who's in control of the final product. OK, is that all clear?'

'Yeah, absolutely,' says Billy, although the truth is that he's confused and starting to feel out of his depth. 'Recipe, script, ingredients, final cut . . .'

'And you're an ingredient,' the Director declares, 'a pinch of something essential.' The Director looks beyond Billy. The Clipboard Lady frowns at him, taps her watch. 'I know, the damned clock is ticking,' the Director mutters. 'Come on,' he says to Billy. 'It's time I did some cooking.'

The Director rams his cigar back in his mouth and strides off.

Billy trots after him, and once again something very strange seems to happen to time. Billy feels he's hardly taken two steps when suddenly he's standing beside the spooky-looking actor – who Billy thought was at least twenty metres away.

Now he's closer to him, Billy can see that the actor's make-up is brilliant, the supposed scars and burnt flesh scarily, eye-poppingly real.

Billy feels a little queasy, realises the Director is talking again.

SLASHER MOVIE

'Let's get down to business,' the Director says. The crew pays attention. Newspapers are folded, conversations come to an end.

'You don't need to know the storyline in detail, Billy,' says the Director. 'It's a slasher movie, plain and simple, and I bet you've seen a few of those, haven't you?'

'I know what a slasher movie is,' Billy murmurs, neglecting to add that he didn't much like the ones he'd seen. They're usually way too gory for him.

'Good, good,' says the Director. 'Well, in this scene, the villain, as played by our friend here, chases you, the victim.' Billy stiffens a little when he hears that. 'You enter running from the left . . .' the Director continues, making a square with his index fingers and thumbs, looking through it as if it's a camera viewfinder, ' . . . and you keep running while we pan. Then you exit from the right, over there.' Billy glances in the direction the Director is pointing, sees he means near the fire escape. 'Got that?' the Director asks.

'I think so,' says Billy, nervous now at what he's being asked to do, his uneasiness focussing on that word 'victim'. 'But that's like, acting, isn't it?' says Billy. 'And you said I wasn't going to do any. I thought an extra just sort of stood in the background . . .'

'I hope you're not going to let me down,' the Director snaps, treating Billy to the same glare he'd given the Clipboard Lady. 'I mean, it's not exactly rocket science, is it? All you've got to do is run, oh, and maybe look scared witless at the same time. You can do that, Billy, can't you?'

Billy is taken aback by the sudden sharpness in the Director's voice, the anger and sarcasm, the abrupt change from the friendliness of a moment ago. He feels a small stirring of anger in himself, a sense that he doesn't want to be talked to in this way, that he doesn't want to be in a film as a victim. It might even be the wrong message to send to Mickey Travis.

Then again, whatever the role, it would still be impressive for him just to be in a film, wouldn't it? Besides, Billy doesn't like thinking how the Director might react if he pulls out now. He has a feeling the Director might give him a seriously hard time. So Billy decides to play along. He takes a deep breath, pushes down his anger, swallows his resentment.

'Yeah, I can do that,' he says. Then something slightly puzzling occurs to him. 'Hey, how do you know my name? I don't think I mentioned it.'

'You must have,' says the Director, all smiles, quickly turning to the crew before Billy can disagree with him. 'Places, everybody. Billy, your mark is on the right, over there,' the Director adds, pointing with his cigar to a small white cross chalked on the

tarmac right beside the scary actor.

The Director returns to his position beside the camera, where a folding canvas chair has suddenly appeared. He sits down in it, holds the script on his lap. The Clipboard Lady is standing next to him, her face blank.

Billy does what he's told, walks over to his mark. He feels more confused than ever. He's sure he didn't tell the Director his name, and now there are a few other things he's beginning to find strange in this whole set-up. For instance, Billy has noticed that no one else seems to be feeling the cold like him. Some of the crew are even wearing Hawaiian shirts with short sleeves.

'Silence on set!' the Clipboard Lady yells,

her voice loud and piercing.

Billy sees a crew member appear in front of him, a man holding up a clapperboard. 'Scene sixty-six, take one!' the man calls out, slamming down the top strip of the clapperboard with a CRACK! like a gunshot.

'Action!' the Director says. Billy looks round – and his blood freezes.

The scary-looking actor isn't motionless any more. In fact, the change in him from stillness to threatening movement happens so fast it's terrifying. He leans forward, ready to spring, the knife raised, its point glinting under the lights, a convincing expression of hate on that hideous face. His cape briefly billows out behind him, flickering red and black.

Then he leaps, and Billy runs, desperate to keep as much distance as possible between himself and that knife. But it's only a film, Billy thinks, part of his

mind registering the crew as he races past them. Yet the sound of pounding feet on the tarmac behind him is real enough. Billy wants to look over his shoulder and daren't. He wonders how close the actor is, how close the blade to the flesh of his back, his soft, vulnerable back . . .

'**CUT!**' a voice yells just as Billy reaches the shadows beneath the fire escape. Billy skids to a halt, worried by the word for a second, then realises it's the Director telling the cameraman to stop filming. Billy looks round, his breath rasping, his heart thudding, sees the actor close behind him. The actor slowly lowers the knife, stares at Billy for a second . . . and hisses.

Then he turns, sweeps his cape around him and stalks away, back to his mark.

Billy uneasily watches him go, feels there is something very unpleasant about him. He's never been hissed at before, not even by Mickey Travis or his thugs.

Suddenly Billy feels the Director standing close beside him.

'Don't worry about your co-star, Billy,' says the Director. 'He's just one of those actors who really likes to get into a part, you know what I mean?'

Billy doesn't know, and he's not sure he cares any more either. And why is the Director referring to the actor as his co-star? Billy's not a star in the movie – he's just an extra, isn't he? This is all too much, Billy thinks, the strangeness, the scariness of the take, the crew staring at him . . .

'Can I go home now?' says Billy. 'That was OK, wasn't it?'

'Well, OK is about right, Billy,' the Director says. 'But I'm pretty sure we can do a hell of a lot better. I want to try another take, only this time –'

'I'm sorry,' Billy mutters. 'I'd really like to help you, but I –'

'Oh, no, I haven't finished with you yet, Billy,' snarls the Director, his voice deepening again to a rumble that makes Billy's head throb. The Director is scowling, his eyes seeming to flash red at Billy for the briefest instant. 'Not by a long way,' he says. 'You'll do exactly what I tell you.'

BLOOD STAIN

Billy is scowling himself now. He's angry with the Director, doesn't like the way he's being treated. He feels like walking round the vans and out of the back gate, forgetting the whole thing. But he sighs, decides to take the line of least resistance, go along with what the Director wants from him.

'OK, then,' says Billy, and shrugs. He slowly walks back to his mark, taking his place beside the spooky actor. He'll just do this one last thing for them, Billy thinks, and then they'll leave him alone. They're bound to.

A happy smile spreads slowly over the Director's face, and Billy notices that the entire crew is definitely smirking at him now. Billy feels more uneasy than ever. What he hears next doesn't make him feel any better.

'Well done, Billy,' says the Director. 'You've passed the test.'

'Test?' says Billy. 'What test? I didn't

know I'd been taking one.'

'Well, you have, Billy,' says the Director, his cigar bobbing up and down as he speaks. 'You've proved you can play the role of a victim. Perfectly.'

'Hey, just hold on a second,' Billy mutters, his anger flooding back.

'Silence on set!' yells the Clipboard Lady. The clapperboard man leaps in front of Billy, grins crazily at him, holds his clapperboard up very close to Billy's face. 'Scene sixty-six – take two!' the man shouts, almost screaming it out, then slams the top section down again and leaps aside.

'Once more, with feeling,' roars the Director. 'OK, Billy – action!'

And suddenly the spooky actor is

moving again. But he doesn't crouch first as he did before, ready to spring – he simply leaps forward, slashing at Billy with the knife. Billy turns and runs, and something happens to time again. Billy feels himself moving slowly, almost as if the air around him has become thick and liquid and resists the motion of his arms and legs.

Billy looks round, and wishes he hadn't. The actor is close behind him, the knife raised, its blade flashing. Billy tears his eyes away, feels a surge of panic, his breath rasping, his heart leaping. The shadows beneath the fire escape are just ahead of him, he has to make it, he's nearly there, three more paces, two more, one more – and then Billy feels a blow to his upper arm.

'CUT!' the Director yells, his voice drawn out, a long, slow groan making that one small word resonate and echo inside Billy's skull.

Billy arrives at the fire escape, skids to a halt, gingerly touches the place where he'd felt the blow, a spot on the back of his upper arm. His jacket there is slashed and, as he explores the torn material, Billy feels a wetness on his fingertips, and simultaneously a sharp pain. Time jolts back into normal speed. He peers at his fingertips, sees a dark stain on them.

He realises it must be blood. His blood. The actor has cut him . . .

Billy stares at the blood for a moment. There's quite a lot of it, although he doesn't think he's been hurt badly. But he shouldn't have been hurt at all, should he? This is a film, and however scary that actor might look, he's still only an actor, isn't he? So what is going on? It has to be a mistake, Billy decides, the stupid man has simply got into his part way too much.

Billy is facing the wall, and suddenly the back of his neck starts prickling the way it does when you have the feeling that you're being stared at. It's strangely quiet behind him too, the only sound the wind whistling softly over the tarmac. Billy is almost too scared to turn round, but he does, and once again this afternoon, his mouth drops open – with sheer terror this time.

The world seems to shift beneath his feet and he feels sick. For the Director, the Clipboard Lady, the entire film crew, all of them have been transformed into creatures from the most terrifying horror movie – the most terrifying nightmare – imaginable. Only the scary actor remains the same, and Billy realises that's because he's not an actor, and he's not made-up. The hideous scars, the burnt flesh, the glinting knife . . . everything is for real. But the scary actor's face is nothing compared to those of the monster crew. Billy closes his eyes, tells himself he must be dreaming, that none of this is happening.

'Oh, but I'm afraid it is, Billy,' he hears the Director say.

Billy wonders if he'd spoken his thoughts aloud, then realises he hadn't. He takes a deep breath of cold air, counts to three, opens his eyes. If anything the scene before him is worse, even more frightening – some of the crew levitating above the lights, cackling as they swoop through the air, a couple diving at him, and up and away again. Billy can feel his heart beating as if it's about to explode, his whole body trembling.

There's no denying the evidence of his senses. And deep down he knows that from the moment he'd walked into this part of the playground he'd felt something wasn't right. But he'd let himself be fooled, hadn't he? Although he can't worry about that now, he tells himself. He needs to find a way out of this. Billy glances round, searching for an escape route, his eyes darting . . .

'Forget it, Billy,' says the Director. 'You're not going anywhere.'

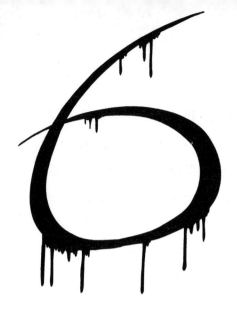

ALL ETERNITY

Billy sees that he's surrounded. He retreats into the shadows beneath the fire escape, but soon finds his back to the wall again, feels the cut in his arm throbbing. Billy presses his shoulder blades against the bricks, wishes he could vanish through them. The creatures are advancing on him.

'Don't come any closer!' he shouts at last. 'You won't get away with this. Someone will see what you're doing from the street. Help! HELP!'

'There's no point calling for help, Billy,' says the Director, laughing softly again, although he does hold his hand up, halting the crew behind him. They stand and stare at Billy, their eyes glowing red. 'The street's a different world,' the Director continues, smiling horribly at him, 'and nobody knows what's happening in here. Nobody but us. And you, of course.'

'But what *is* happening?' Billy asks, trying his hardest to stay calm, to keep his voice steady. 'I don't understand. Who are you? What are you?'

'So many questions, Billy,' says the Director. 'Let's just say that we're not the people you thought we were, although I think we gave an excellent performance, don't you? But then we've had plenty of practice at this sort of thing. You could call us spirits. Or maybe demons is a better word.'

The creatures smirk, and Billy feels his stomach tighten.

'OK, I believe you,' he mutters. 'But what do you want with me?

'I've already told you,' says the Director. 'I just want you to be in my movie, that's all. The script demands a victim – and you're so good at being one. That's the reason we were drawn to you in the first place.'

'What are you talking about?' Billy's voice is small and quiet.

'It's just like your chum Mickey said,' the Director murmurs, and his face flickers, morphing into Mickey's face while

he speaks, his voice into Mickey's voice. *'You're a born loser, pal. It's written all over you, and you'll never, ever change . . .'* The Director becomes his hideous self again, smiles at Billy. 'Mind you, I had to be sure,' he says. 'So I kept pushing you, bullying you into doing what I wanted you to do. And you passed the test.'

Suddenly Billy finds himself thinking about Mickey. And now he realises with a shock that Mickey had been testing him too, seeing how far he could push him. It all falls into place. Billy sees that he'd looked like a loser to Mickey for one very simple reason – he had always acted like one. Going along with what Mickey was doing, not causing any trouble, even hiding . . .

He should have drawn the line from the start, thinks Billy, whatever the consequences. Suddenly Billy feels angry with himself for putting up with someone like Mickey Travis – for letting a lowlife like Mickey bully him. The anger swiftly replaces his fear, and he stops trembling.

'Well, I'm still not convinced he's right for the part,' the Clipboard Lady is saying, her voice the same, her face a mask of horror. 'I mean, he can't be very bright if he fell for all that awful guff you came out with about making a movie being like making a

69

cake. I don't know how I kept a straight face.'

'I thought it was rather clever,' the Director snaps at her, several of the crew sniggering at him behind his back. 'Anyway, he doesn't need to be bright, does he? As I said, he just needs to run and be scared witless, and he does that brilliantly. Right, that's enough chitchat. Time for another take . . .'

'Hold on,' says Billy, his attention returning to what's happening around him. 'You expect me to let that creature chase me again, like he did before?'

'Oh yes, Billy,' says the Director, grinning happily. 'In fact, I expect you to let him chase you again and again and again, only he's going to catch you every time and do nasty, gory things to you. And when we get bored with that scenario, we'll think of something else equally terrifying . . . You're going to become very familiar with the word CUT!, and we're going to have so much fun watching you suffer . . . for all eternity. OK, places everybody!'

And Billy instantly finds himself standing on his white cross once more.

The crew cackle and rub their hands together as they do what they're told.

The scary actor takes up his position, raises his knife, gives Billy a chilling little wave, mimes a few slashing movements as though he's warming up. The Director sits in his folding chair, the script on his lap, the Clipboard Lady beside him. Billy frowns, hates the way they sit there looking smug.

'Silence on set!' the Clipboard Lady calls out. The creature with the clapperboard capers madly in front of Billy. 'Scene sixty-six, take three!' he yells.

But Billy pushes past him before he can slam the top of the clapperboard down, before the Director can say 'Action!' and start the nightmare rolling.

'NO!' Billy shouts at the top of his voice. 'I WON'T DO IT!'

FINAL CUT

The crew's smiles vanish as Billy's words echo around them. Suddenly the wind picks up, whistling through this small section of playground, ruffling clothes and hair. The Director slowly rises from his chair, puts the script down on it behind him, walks forward a few paces. He stares hard at Billy.

'Don't be silly, Billy,' says the Director. 'You've got no choice.'

'Yes I have,' says Billy. 'And I choose not to make it easy for you. I choose not to go along with what you want. I choose to spoil your fun!'

'Ah, but you're forgetting one thing, Billy,' says the Director. 'It's all written in the script, and you'll never change it. You're my victim now.'

'Is that right?' says Billy, his anger suddenly turning into a cold fury. The Director's words have also given him an idea. Billy suddenly dashes forward, runs through the crew before any of them can grab him, dodges round the Director – and finally reaches his chair.

Billy grabs the script, sits down in the chair with it on his lap.

The head of every creature there swivels in unison to stare at him, and a low wail issues from their throats. The sound blends with the wind's moan.

'Give it to me, Billy,' the Director says. 'Give it to me now.'

Billy looks at the Director, notices that he seems, well . . . worried.

'I don't think I will,' Billy replies, realising that he's definitely on to something. 'I want to see exactly what is written in this script of yours.'

Billy opens it, flicks through, is amazed. The script begins with a scene in the boys'

toilets featuring characters called Billy
Gibson and Mickey Travis and
Tweedledum and Tweedledee. Then the
character called Billy emerges from the
school, sees a film crew, talks to somebody
called the Director . . . It was all there,

everything that had happened to him since he'd hidden in the boys' toilets. And there were more pages, more lines beyond the last ones he'd spoken, scenes that made Billy wince as his eyes skimmed over them.

But a line early in the script had caught Billy's eye, something about a red biro. Billy reaches into his pocket, pulls out the pen, stares at it for a moment. He hears another wail. He glances up at the faces watching him.

Now they're actually looking terrified, every one of them – the Director, the Clipboard Lady, the actor with the knife, the whole damned crew. And so they should be, thinks Billy. He smiles, leans back in the chair, taps the script with the pen. He's good at writing stories, isn't he? So why shouldn't he change this one, cross out what was coming, give it a different ending?

'I don't like this script,' says Billy. The wail grows in volume and intensity. 'I can't do much about what's already happened. But I can

certainly make sure I like what happens next, can't I?' He pulls off the biro top, opens the script at the point they'd reached, scores a red line across the page, across the next one, and the next, finally ripping pages out, screwing them up and throwing them down. But the last one is blank, and Billy holds on to it, smoothes it out on the rest of the script. He thinks for a second.

Then he begins to write, saying the words aloud as he scribbles them down.

'Billy sits in the Director's chair, and suddenly the nightmare film crew starts to fade, then vanish, one by one. The same happens to the vans and equipment and even the torn-out pages of script, to the scary actor, to the Clipboard Lady, until only the Director is left. He stands motionless, a shrunken, pathetic figure, a bogeyman who isn't frightening any more.

Billy stops writing, looks at the Director one last time.

'I'd like to say it's been nice knowing you,' says Billy. 'But it hasn't.'

Billy looks down and writes on, the words coming quickly now as he hurries to the end. 'The Director himself starts to fade. He shakes his fist at Billy, but it's

too late. The Director vanishes with a faint POP!, the air rushing in to fill the space he's been occupying, the burning red tip of his cigar the last part of him to disappear.'

Billy sighs, stops writing, folds the piece of paper and puts it in his jacket pocket along with the pen.

Billy stands, the chair vanishes, the air shimmering around him for a moment. The wind whistles softly over the empty tarmac, and he raises his head, looks up at the sky. It's free of clouds. A few lonely

stars glitter above the school, the playground, the back gate. Time to go home, thinks Billy. He walks away, notices that his arm isn't throbbing any more, that his sleeve isn't slashed. He pauses, wonders briefly if it had all happened.

Then Billy realises he's still holding the script, the part he didn't rip out and throw away. So there's no doubting it. He walks

on, stops by the back gate. Beside it is a small rubbish bin. It's usually stuffed with sweet wrappers and crushed drink cans, but tonight it's empty.

Billy looks at the wodge of paper – then rams it in the bin. Good riddance, he thinks, and goes out through the gate, into the street. He's still got the pen, though, so he knows he can write another film. A much better one, in which he tells his mum and dad and his teachers about Mickey, makes them believe him and do something. A movie in which he stands up to Mickey.

If he can deal with the Director, he can deal with anybody.

Billy Gibson is the only person who's going to be in control of his movie in future. He's the one who'll have final cut. Billy turns the corner, stops, takes a deep breath, lets it out, feels the tension drain away. Billy smiles.

He is really, really looking forward to school tomorrow.

VOODOO CHILD

CONTENTS

ONE: FADING LIGHT

Find a pin and stick it in.
Find a pin and stick it in . . .

Megan spotted the sign as soon as she came round the corner from the main road. She kept walking along the street in the fading November light, her eyes fixed on the square board at the top of the tall, white-painted post standing beside her gate. It hadn't been there when she'd left for school that morning, but she had a nasty feeling she knew what kind of sign it was.

She stopped by the gate and looked up. FOR SALE, the sign said in large letters. Below them were the name and phone number of an estate agent.

Megan scowled. She pushed through the gate and stomped down the path to the house. She fumbled her key out of her coat pocket, opened the door, went into the hall and slammed it behind her. She dumped her schoolbag at the bottom of the stairs. 'Mum!' she yelled. 'Mum, where are you?'

The kitchen was empty, the back door

wide open, and Megan went into the garden. Her mother was raking fallen leaves, piling them up on the scruffy patch of grass they called the lawn. Mum turned and smiled at her.

'Why is that sign outside?' Megan said. 'You didn't tell me anything about selling the house. You can't do it. I won't let you!'

'I told you last week the estate agent was coming,' Mum said, her smile faltering. Her dark hair was in a ponytail, and she was wearing jeans tucked into Wellington boots, and an old hooded coat. 'You chose to ignore me, that's all. I know it's hard for you, but we simply can't put it off any more.'

'I don't want to move,' said Megan, her scowl deepening, her voice as determined

3

as she could make it sound. 'I've lived here my whole life.'

'But things have changed, Megan,' said Mum. She started raking leaves again, her movements brisk and busy. 'This house is too big for just the two of us, and it's certainly far too expensive for me to run on my own. And now that your father and I have decided to get a . . .'

'I'm not listening!' Megan yelled, clamping her hands over her ears. She knew Mum's next word would be 'divorce', and she couldn't bear to hear it.

Mum stopped raking and looked round. 'Oh, Megan,' she said, reaching out to touch her daughter's cheek.

'You're going to have to get used to the idea some time, love. It doesn't have to be the end of the world, does it?'

'It might be for me,' said Megan, uncovering her ears and swaying back to avoid her mother's hand. 'But then nobody cares what I think, do they?'

They stood in silence for a moment, the sky above them darkening with clouds the deep purple of fresh bruises, the chill autumn air laced with the faint smoky smell of old bonfires. Megan shivered, and crossed her arms.

5

'I care,' Mum said. 'In fact, I'm worried about you. You never see your friends any more, you sit in that room of yours too much, and you seem so . . . angry all the time.' She waited for Megan to say something, but Megan stayed silent. 'OK,' Mum said. 'Let me finish out here, then we'll sit down and have a little chat, like we used to when you came home from school. You go and get changed and put the kettle on. I could murder a cup of tea.'

'I don't want a little chat,' Megan snapped. 'I've got homework to do.'

She turned on her heel and marched into the house. She took off her coat and slung it over the banisters, grabbed her bag, stomped upstairs, barged into her room. She dropped her bag and sat at her desk, jabbing the 'Power' button of her stereo system. The radio was tuned to her favourite station, and music flowed from the speakers – the current single by a boy band she liked.

But Megan barely paid attention to it, the sweet, smooth voices a mere background murmur to the furious thoughts filling her mind. 'Things have changed,' Mum had said. They certainly have, Megan brooded. Angry? You bet she was angry. After what had happened, she had a perfect right to be.

Until a year before, Megan had believed they were a happy family. Of course, her parents had been moody with each other sometimes, and argued quite a lot. But all mums and dads argued, didn't

they? Then the rows had suddenly got worse, and one terrible week they had gone on and on – until they had ended with Dad walking out. At the time, Mum had been too upset to tell Megan much. But what she had said had been more than enough.

Dad had a girlfriend; someone at his office. A woman called Sarah.

Megan remembered how she'd felt when she had first heard that name – shocked, disbelieving, hurt and, yes, angry. Very angry. It was several weeks before she could speak to her father on the phone, a couple of months before she would agree to see him, although he took her out most weekends now, to see a film, to eat at MacDonald's, sometimes just to sit in the park and talk.

Not that Megan said much. She grunted single word replies to Dad's questions about school, and said nothing when he talked about Sarah.

And he did, a lot. Megan had wondered why he kept bringing her into the conversation; then gradually she'd begun to realise Dad wanted her to meet his girlfriend. But he'd only got the courage up a few times to ask, and so far Megan had responded with a look that said 'How dare you?' She was sure things would never have changed if it hadn't been for . . . that woman.

Megan had seen her once. Dad had returned to collect more of his stuff, and Sarah had sat outside in the car. Megan had hidden upstairs and peeked from behind a curtain. She'd studied Sarah's tense profile, the pretty face, the pink lips and dyed blonde hair burning themselves into her memory.

'So you'd like to get back at her?' a voice said, breaking into her thoughts. She wondered where the voice had come from, then realised it must be the DJ on the radio, the one who hosted an after-school phone-in. Megan thought she was cool, and her show was always interesting – people calling in to talk about problems with their parents or teachers or friends.

Megan stood up and started to change

out of her school uniform.

'Yes, I would,' a girl said, her voice bitter. 'She's been so mean I've even been thinking of making a doll that looks like her and sticking pins in it.'

'Whoa, a bit of the old voodoo magic!' said the DJ, laughing. 'Well, that won't make her want to be your best friend again, but if it helps you feel better . . .'

Megan was standing before the full-length mirror on her wardrobe, and paused halfway through pulling a sweater over her head. She'd just had a vision of a doll made to look exactly like Sarah, a doll bristling with pins. Megan finished putting on the sweater, flicked her long dark hair out of the collar with a quick motion of her hands. She looked into her green eyes in the mirror – and, for an instant, they seemed to flash a fiery, scary yellow.

Megan was startled, and stepped back. She blinked and rubbed her eyes, then opened them, and cautiously looked in the mirror again. But the yellow had gone and her eyes had reverted to their normal colour. She glanced round and saw that the window blind was raised, the last rays of the setting sun shining over the roofs of the houses on the other side of the street.

It must have been a reflection, Megan decided, a flash of sunlight in the mirror. But it had been oddly disturbing. And something else was bothering her too. She couldn't get that image of the Sarah doll out of her mind . . .

TWO: MIDNIGHT MAGIC

At supper that evening Mum tried again to talk about moving. They were sitting at their usual places in the kitchen, Mum at one end of the old pine table, Megan at the side, next to her, facing the place where her father had always sat. But his chair was empty, as it had been for the last year.

'We'll probably only be able to afford a flat,' Mum was saying. 'Still, the estate agent said we should be able to find something nice, maybe on the ground floor with two bedrooms and a garden. She left me some details. We could have a look at them later if you like, see what you think.'

'You already know what I think,' Megan muttered, poking at the pasta with her fork, refusing to meet her mother's gaze. 'I don't want to move.'

Mum put down her own fork and sighed. 'I'm sorry, Megan,' she said quietly, 'but it's going to happen whether you want it to or not. Listen, I'm sure it's the right thing for both of us. I wouldn't be doing it otherwise.'

'Fine,' said Megan, and shrugged. She raised her head, looked her mother in the eyes. 'Go ahead then. Just don't expect me to like the idea.'

Mum didn't speak for a second, her eyes locked on to her daughter's. 'OK, love,' she said at last. 'Have it your way. I know you're upset about what's happened. So am I, although I had a feeling it was coming . . . But remember, you won't ever be happy again till you stop being angry. And that's what I want. I want my old Megan back – my happy, smiling, laughing Megan.'

Megan dropped her fork into her bowl and pushed it away. 'Can I get down from the table, please?' she said. 'I'm not hungry.' She didn't wait for an answer, but immediately stood up and marched out of the kitchen.

It was dark in the hall, darker still on the upstairs landing. Megan went into her room, and was glad that she'd left the bedside lamp on earlier, its warm, golden glow keeping the shadows penned in the room's corners.

She hit the stereo system's 'Power' switch, then lay on the bed. She took a book from the bedside table, but didn't open it. She was even angrier now. She would love to be the Megan her mother had described. She was fed up with being miserable, wished she was happy again. But her old life had been stolen from her, and all her happiness and laughter had been taken along with it. And she could think of nothing that might make her feel better.

Then suddenly that image of the Sarah doll bobbed up to the surface of her mind, and the DJ's words along with it. A bit of the old voodoo magic . . .

'Voodoo,' Megan murmured. She liked the sound of the word, the buzz of the 'V' between her front teeth and bottom lip, the spooky 'oo's separated and at the same time linked by the 'd'. But apart from a few vague memories of things she'd seen in films, she didn't really know what it meant.

Megan put her book down, swung her legs off the bed and went over to the desk. Next to the stereo were the monitor and keyboard of a computer, a recent present from her father. She knew he'd bought it out of guilt, so she'd barely used it. She remembered that it had come with a range of CDs, mostly games she'd never play. But there was an encyclopaedia too.

She switched on the computer, found the right CD case, loaded the disk in the stack under her desk. Soon she was

reading the entry headed 'Voodoo'.

'Religion developed in the Caribbean by Africans taken there as slaves . . . mixture of African and Christian elements . . . often depicted in horror movies as sorcery, a magical means to harm enemies . . .' She searched for a mention of voodoo dolls. 'Figures made in the likeness of someone into which pins can be stuck, supposedly to inflict pain on an enemy, or to cause death . . .'

She had come to the end of the entry. Megan sat still for a moment, her face bathed in the pale blue light of the monitor, her hand poised on the mouse.

Then she smiled and thought, Why not? It would be simple enough, she was sure. All she needed was an old doll to work with, and she had a few of those. And it would just be a bit of fun, a little game to make her feel better.

Yes, do it, do it, a voice hissed in her ear. *Hurt her, hurt her!*

Megan looked round at the radio, but she knew the voice wasn't coming from there. It was as if someone else was in the room with her, someone invisible. She closed her eyes and shook her head, but the voice persisted, buzzing in her other ear now like an irritating insect, repeating the same words, *Hurt her, hurt her, hurt her* . . . until at last she clamped her hands over both ears – and the voice stopped. Megan opened her eyes and took a deep breath. Then she sat up, breathed out, decided she must have imagined it.

Although for a second the voice had seemed very real.

Mum checked on her later, said it was time she turned off the radio and got into bed. Megan went to the bathroom and cleaned her teeth. Back in her room she changed into her pyjamas and slid beneath the duvet. She tried to read, but her mind was racing. After a while she realised she'd been stuck on the same sentence for five minutes, and put her book down once more.

Megan switched off the lamp, as she usually did. The shadows in the corners of the room leapt out and merged into a velvety blackness, the only light coming from the green numerals of her alarm clock and the winking dots between them. It was always like that, of course. But tonight it was somehow far too dark, and she sat up and switched the lamp back on.

She thought for a moment.

'Oh, why not?' she muttered.

11:45

She got out of bed and tiptoed over to a large basket standing beside the wardrobe. Mum called it The Junk Basket, because Megan kept in it all the things she couldn't bear to throw away – her old toys and games, souvenirs from outings and holidays, diaries and letters, even her old exercise books.

She started rummaging, doing it quietly so Mum wouldn't hear. Megan knew exactly what she was looking for, and it didn't take long to find it.

She sat at the desk to examine the object of her search. It was a small cloth doll, one she remembered playing with when she'd been very young. It didn't have a name like most of the other dolls she'd hung on to, and it wasn't particularly special. It still wore the original blue dress it had come in, and it had an almost blank face, the eyes no more than black dots; a downward line and two smaller dots to suggest a nose, a short, horizontal line for a mouth. But, more importantly, it had nylon hair that was just the right length and colour. The same length and colour as Sarah's.

Megan held the doll in her hand. And almost before she knew what she was doing, she had opened the desk drawer and grabbed a fistful of felt-tip pens. She used a black one to give the doll eyebrows; pink to create a pair of pouting, rosebud lips. She fluffed out the blonde hair. Then she pulled up the dress and wrote SARAH in bright, blood red, right across the doll's body.

Megan stared at the spiky letters on the white fabric. She told herself how silly it all was, and laughed. But it was a nervous, uneasy laugh, because part of her felt this wasn't a game, that it was a very strange thing to be doing.

Then she heard the voice hissing in her ear once more, the words hard to make out at first. But they soon grew louder, clearer, easier to understand.

26

Find a pin and stick it in, the voice was saying. *Find a pin and stick it in.*

Megan felt compelled to do what the voice said. She looked in the drawer, saw a badge from an old birthday card. She picked it up, turned it over, bent the pin away from the metal circle till it stood out straight, like a tiny dagger.

Suddenly, from the corner of an eye, Megan thought she saw movement beyond her bed, in the darkest corner of the room, and a flash of burning yellow in the blackness. She turned round, her heart fluttering, her throat tight. But there was nothing there, only the deep, thick, velvety shadows.

Her eyes were drawn to the flashing dots between the green numerals on the alarm clock. As she watched, the numbers changed from 11.59 p.m. to 12.00 a.m.

It's midnight, the time for magic, she thought, a part of her still detached, wondering why she was behaving so bizarrely. But the voice kept on. *Stick it in, stick it in, stick it in.* The shadows in the room seemed to gather round her, and Megan felt her arms and legs trembling again.

In, in, in . . .

She jammed the pin into the doll's fabric stomach as hard as she could. To her horror, the doll seemed to squirm in her hand and she dropped it.

Then a flood of darkness filled her mind and she knew no more.

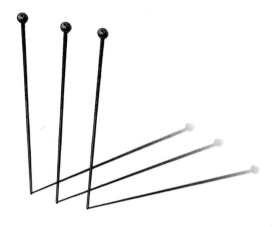

THREE: DARK THOUGHTS

Light. Pale, weak, morning light seeping round the edges of the plain, cream-coloured blind pulled down over the window. Megan's alarm clock had bleeped, but she lay stiffly in bed, unable to enjoy the cosy warmth beneath the duvet, those few, usually delicious moments before she had to get up for school. She felt tense, wondered if she'd had a bad dream.

Then she remembered. The Sarah doll; the shadows in the corners of the room; the voice telling her to stick the pin in. With a shiver of renewed horror, Megan remembered the doll squirming in her hand as she'd done it. Or maybe she'd dreamed that, she thought. In fact, maybe the whole thing had been a nightmare after all. But then she glanced over at the desk.

The doll was lying where she must have dropped it the night before, on the desk beside the stereo, the pin of the badge buried deep in its stomach.

Megan got out of bed and stood staring at the doll. Her room was warm – the heating came on early at this time of year – but she was shivering even more now. She took a deep breath, yanked the badge free and threw it in the drawer, grabbed the doll and stuffed it into The Junk Basket, dumped the lid on top. Then she jumped back into bed and tried to stop herself shivering.

'Megan!' she heard Mum call from downstairs. 'Your breakfast is ready!'

Megan relaxed a little, felt the tremors begin to subside. The familiarity of Mum's voice anchored things, drove the memories away. Voodoo dolls weren't part of the ordinary world where mums called

31

daughters for breakfast, were they? Why had she got herself into such a state?

She slipped out of bed, put on her dressing gown, hurried downstairs.

It was bright and noisy and completely normal in the kitchen, the kettle boiling, the toaster popping, Mum humming along to the radio, eating her breakfast before she went to work. By the time Megan said goodbye and left for school, she had almost forgotten the doll and what she had done to it.

Almost, but not quite. A shadowy image of the doll hovered at the edge of her mind and, as the day went by, Megan had to concentrate harder and harder to keep it at bay. Whenever she let that concentration slip – if her attention wandered during a boring lesson, for instance – the image instantly grew stronger, the voice hissing and buzzing and whining in her ears.

She could barely think of anything else on her way home. Dark thoughts filled her mind, visions of sticking pins in the doll and what that might do to her father's girlfriend, the images accompanied by fierce pleasure. But there were other feelings too – fear, and a sense that she might be on the edge of doing something wrong. The sky was closing in as she turned into her street, thick clouds lit red underneath by the sun behind the houses, a whispering breeze chasing leaves around her feet and along the pavement in front of her.

Megan went through the gate, her eyes averted from the sign. She walked down the path, opened the front door. Mum wasn't home yet, and it was quiet and still inside the house. Megan took off her coat and hung it up, went into the kitchen, made a sandwich, poured herself a glass of cold milk. She took her snack upstairs to her room, put the plate and glass on the desk, dropped her bag on the bed. She was going to eat her sandwich, drink the milk, then get on with her homework. But she didn't do any of that.

Instead, she found herself standing beside The Junk Basket.

I won't lift the lid, she decided. Then she realised she had done just that, and there was the doll, lying face up on top of everything else inside, even though Megan remembered ramming it in, pushing it down beneath all the other stuff. She sensed that the doll was staring up at her. Waiting.

The voice started hissing again in Megan's ear.

Pick it up, pick it up, pick it up.

Megan did as she was told. She held the doll in her hand. It was exactly as she remembered, the black eyebrows, the pink lips, the blood-red letters on the body spelling SARAH. Although now it also had a tiny hole in the fabric of its stomach. Megan brushed a fingertip across the hole, wondered if it really was possible to hurt someone by jabbing a pin into a doll . . .

Suddenly she felt she simply had to

know – and there was only one way to find out.

She pulled her mobile out of her bag, called her father at his office.

'Well, this is a lovely surprise,' Dad said when she was put through to him. 'You don't usually phone me here. What's brought this on then?'

'I don't know,' said Megan. 'I just felt like a chat, I suppose.' She kept her voice light, tried to talk in the way she'd always done before he left.

'Hey, that's great,' said Dad.

She could tell that he was pleased, and she realised he probably thought she was beginning to ease up on him. But she didn't care about that. He could think what he liked. All she was interested in was his girlfriend.

'So – how's school going this week?' Dad said.

'School's OK,' said Megan. 'But I was wondering – how's . . . Sarah?'

There was a profound silence at the other end of the line. Megan had never used Sarah's name in a conversation with her father before, not once, and for a second she thought she might have gone too far, that Dad had somehow worked out she must have a sinister reason for asking after her.

'Nice of you to ask,' Dad said eventually, and to Megan's relief he sounded even more pleased than he had done before. But there was some worry in his voice too, and a little puzzlement.

'She was a bit poorly last night, actually. She woke up about midnight with a pretty bad stomach ache. It kept her awake most of the night, but then this morning the pain just vanished, and she seems fine now. Anyway, I'd better go. I've got lots to do . . . no rest for the wicked, eh? See you at the weekend, love. I thought we could try that new ice cream place in town; if it's all right with you . . .'

'Yeah . . . sure, Dad,' Megan mumbled, her mind suddenly in turmoil.

They said their goodbyes and Megan hurriedly ended the call. She sat on the bed, still holding the doll in her hand. She stared at it, and felt her skin crawl. The thought that the magic might actually have worked scared her and made her feel guilty too. But it also made her excited.

It was then that she heard the voice again. It had returned, was urging her to try again, to do something else to the Sarah doll.

Do it, do it, do it. Hurt her, hurt her, hurt her . . .

Megan did her best to resist it. She decided to go downstairs, watch TV for a while. Maybe that would get this crazy nonsense out of her mind.

An instant later she was in her mother's bedroom, searching through the dresser drawer where Mum kept her sewing things. Megan found what she was after – a little box she remembered seeing when

Mum had altered her school dress at the beginning of term. Megan took the box out, opened it.

The silver pins inside slithered and rustled as if they were alive.

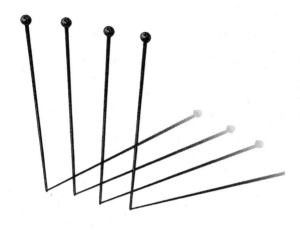

FOUR: SHADOW CREATURE

'Come on, Megan,' said Mum. 'I really think it's time you went to bed.'

Megan was sitting in the corner of the big sofa in the front room, beneath the glare of the main light. She was hugging a cushion, watching TV with the sound up loud, a detective story she'd seen before, although that didn't matter. It had been keeping her mind occupied, stopping her from thinking.

'Do I have to?' she muttered. 'I want to know what happens in this.'

'It's late, and you've got school tomorrow,' said Mum. She was standing over Megan, hands on hips. 'Anyway, you do know what's going to happen. We watched it a few months ago, remember? So no more argument, please.'

Megan sighed dramatically, tossed the cushion aside and jumped to her feet. She brushed past her mother, went into the dimly lit hall, ran upstairs. She paused on the landing outside her room, reluctant to go in, listening as Mum lowered the

TV's volume and changed channels. Then Megan turned, took a deep breath, quickly went inside, and closed the door behind her.

She stood with her back against it. She had left the lamp on as before, but this time the shadows in the corners were pressing in on its golden glow, eagerly waiting to drown it in their thick blackness. Megan didn't want to look at the dark, keeping her eyes firmly on the lit area – on her desk.

The box of pins was still where she had left it, next to the stereo.

Megan shuddered, had one of those small, harmless trembling fits that Mum always said meant someone was walking over your grave. She remembered how earlier that evening she had brought the box of pins back to her room, how she had felt an urge to start sticking pins into the Sarah doll immediately. And how hard it had been to stop herself. The sense of compulsion, of being under the control of a force she didn't understand, had been so scary. But it had been thrilling too.

And then the voice had returned, harsher and more insistent; it hadn't even stopped when she'd clamped her hands over her ears. Megan had finally fled from her room, putting a couple of closed doors between herself and the box of pins and the doll, which she had stuffed in The Junk Basket again. It had worked for a while, Mum's chatter about her day keeping the voice at bay, the TV drowning it out. But

Megan had known the voice was just below the threshold of her awareness, waiting to make itself heard. Now she was back in her room it was already faintly there.

Megan gritted her teeth and went to the desk. She opened the drawer, swept the box of pins inside, slammed the drawer shut. She jabbed the 'Power' button on the stereo and started getting ready for bed, humming along to the music as she changed into her pyjamas, trying to keep her mind on anything but the doll and the pins and the voice. She went to the bathroom, brushed her teeth, returned to her room, got into bed. She picked up a book, forced herself to read, turned the pages, made her eyes follow the sentences.

As usual, Mum looked in on her a little later, told her to switch off the stereo, said goodnight. Megan heard her go into her own bedroom and close the door. And suddenly the house was full of brooding, crackling silence, the air in Megan's room thick with it. She sat stiffly in bed, listening, feeling her heart thump in her chest, the blood pulsing through her body. The voice was in her ears, the hissing becoming words that couldn't be clearer.

46

Get the doll, get the doll, get the doll. Hurt her, hurt her, hurt her . . .

Megan realised she was standing beside The Junk Basket, and didn't know how she'd got there. She lifted the lid. The doll was lying where she had left it. Megan didn't want to pick it up, but she couldn't stop herself reaching out towards it. The doll leapt into her hand. The shadows swirled beyond the glow of the lamp and Megan swayed. She closed her eyes and when she opened them she was sitting at the desk, the doll squirming in her grasp, the box of pins open in front of her, the pins rustling and gleaming.

Stick them in, stick them in, stick them in . . .

Now Megan had a pin in her other hand. She rolled the cool, slender piece of silver metal between the tip of her forefinger and thumb, studied it in the light of the lamp, her eyes zooming in like a camera on the sharp, glinting point. She squeezed the pin tight in her fingers, bit her lip, felt herself slowly drawing her hand back . . . and stopped, resisting the urge to stick it in.

But it was hard, so hard, and her hand and arm began to tremble.

Hurt her, said the voice. *HURT HER, HURT HER, HURT HER!*

It sounded more real now, as if it were coming from another person in the room. Megan turned, looked into the darkest corner, and someone – or something – was there. At first, all she could see was an outline, a dark figure only separated from the shadows around it by its thicker blackness. Then two bright dots winked

into existence near the head of the figure.

A pair of fiery yellow eyes was staring back at her.

She saw that the figure was person-shaped, and the size of a child. But it was like a shadow given substance, a creature made of darkness solidified, with no features other than those staring, burning eyes. Megan felt a peculiar sensation at the back of her neck and realised it was true, the hairs there did stand up when you were scared. And Megan was more

frightened than she'd ever been in her life before – although there was that thrill of excitement in the fear too.

Why won't you do it? the figure hissed at last. It moved, flowed out of the corner of the room towards her. It stood beside the desk like a dark spectre, those fiery yellow eyes fixed on hers. *You know you really want to.*

'I can't,' said Megan, wondering why she was speaking to this shadow creature. Then she realised that it felt right, that she had been waiting a long time to have such a conversation. 'It's wrong to hurt someone . . . isn't it?'

That's just your conscience talking, the figure hissed. Megan could see a hole beneath the eyes now, a thin mouth that moved as the voice spoke. *SHE didn't think twice about hurting you, did she? You should get back at her!*

'But it's not the same, is it?' said Megan. 'I mean, the doll . . . the pins . . .'

Of course it is! the figure said, drifting even closer, the dark mouth almost touching Megan's ear. *Pain is pain, and she deserves everything she gets. Hurt her, hurt her, hurt her! There's no limit to what you can do, either.*

'What do you mean?' said Megan, a cold chill running up her spine.

Think about it, said the shadow creature. *Just one pin in the doll gave her a stomach ache that lasted till you took the pin out. So what might LOTS of pins do to her? Pins in the doll's stomach, pins in its head, one in its heart . . .*

'That might . . . kill her!' whispered Megan. 'No, I couldn't do it . . .'

Why not? the shadow creature snapped. Its voice almost seemed to be coming from deep inside Megan's head now. *What are you worried about? No one will ever suspect you. Besides, if you get rid of his girlfriend, Dad will come back and life will be the same as it was before, before, before . . .*

Megan sat there, the last word echoing in her mind. She was still holding the doll in one hand, the pin in the other. She was tempted, very tempted . . .

Then she heard a noise on the landing outside her bedroom. The voice instantly fell silent and Megan felt as if a spell had been broken. She came to her senses, looked over her shoulder, saw that the door was opening. She dropped the pin on the desk and hurriedly got back into bed, pushing the doll beneath the duvet to hide it, grabbing the book from the bedside table.

The shadow creature had vanished as if it had never existed.

Mum's face appeared round the door. 'Are you OK?' she said.

'I'm fine,' said Megan. 'I just couldn't sleep, that's all.'

'I thought I heard you talking,' said Mum, looking puzzled.

'I wasn't,' said Megan. 'Maybe . . . maybe you imagined it.'

Mum seemed satisfied. As soon as she was gone, Megan jumped out of bed and returned the doll to The Junk Basket. Then she got back into bed, and lay there wondering if she had been the one doing the imagining. But the voice soon returned. *Life will be the same as it was before, before, before . . .*

That night, Megan dreamed of dolls and pins and shadow creatures – and other things too. She dreamed of unbearable pain, and murder, and death.

Death darker than the shadows in her room. Much darker.

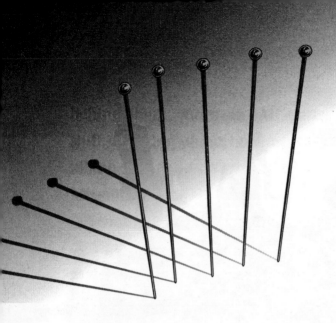

FIVE: DEEPENING DARKNESS

The next day was a Friday, a school day like any other. Megan sat in her lessons, did what she had to, answered if she was spoken to. But her mind was full of what had happened the night before, and she could hardly wait for the day to end. It did at last, and she was first out of the school gates.

It was drizzling, and the late afternoon sky was a ceiling of thick, purple-grey clouds, their bulging, damp undersides pressing down on the roofs of the houses Megan passed. Some of the cars swishing by already had their headlights on, and the beams were weak against the deepening darkness.

Mum was in when she got home, but Megan barely acknowledged her greeting. She took off her coat and went straight upstairs to her bedroom.

She dumped her schoolbag, opened the desk drawer and got out the badge and box of pins. She went over to The Junk Basket and took out the Sarah doll. Sitting cross-legged on the bed, she put the badge and the box of pins and the doll on the duvet in front of her, carefully positioning them.

Megan studied the three objects closely. Then she leaned back and sighed.

She had decided to ask herself a simple question. Was she going mad? In the light of day it had been hard to believe in the voice and the creature that seemed to have appeared in her room – hard to believe that she had inflicted pain on someone by sticking a pin in a doll. If it hadn't happened – if it had been a dream or imagination, and Sarah's pain that night just a coincidence – then yes, she was going mad. Not just a bit mad either. She must be totally crazy. But none of it

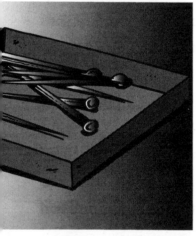

had seemed like a dream . . . and now she was in her room with the badge and the box of pins and the doll in front of her, the memory of how she had felt flooded through her again, that exhilarating mixture of fear and excitement. Those feelings had been real enough, she thought. And it had all seemed to make sense as well. A deeply satisfying kind of sense.

Megan looked up. Her window blind was raised, so she could see that the sky was almost black now. The shadows in the room were as thick as usual, and there was a hissing in her ears. She didn't have to listen to know what the voice was saying, to know that the voice was real, that somehow she'd managed to conjure up a demon. A voodoo child. Yes, that was what she'd call it, she thought, shivering as she remembered that dark figure. She wondered where it had come from, why conjuring it up had been so easy.

Did the voodoo child give the doll its magic? Or did sticking pins in the doll unleash the voodoo child? . . . Although none of that really mattered. Not compared to the choice the voodoo child had offered her last night . . .

Megan picked up the box of pins, opened it, took a couple out, held them in the palm of her hand. She looked at the doll, thought about sticking a pin in the place where a person's heart would be. Could it be that simple? Would it really kill Sarah? And if it worked, could she live with herself afterwards?

Yes, the voice suddenly hissed inside her head. *If Dad came back and life was the same as it was before, before, before . . .*

Megan closed her eyes for a second, listened to the voice, felt it pulling her deep into a pool of darkness somewhere inside her. Why not give in to it? Why not get rid of Sarah once and for all? It would be so good, Megan thought, so very, very satisfying . . .

There was another voice in her head too, but Megan refused to let her conscience have its say. She opened her eyes, looked down at the pins in her palm, barely visible in the gloom of the room. She rolled them to and fro and smiled, beginning to enjoy the sense that she was in control, that she was powerful and

dangerous. Yes, she would do it, she decided. Perhaps she should even do it now, right this second, get it over with . . .

Suddenly she heard footsteps outside her door, and she froze. Mum was crossing the landing.

Megan held her breath, heard Mum going downstairs. She relaxed, but decided to do the magic later. At midnight, of course. It would be much safer then, with Mum tucked up in bed and unlikely to walk in and catch her.

Megan put the pins back in the box, rose from the bed and switched on the lamp, the shadows scurrying away from its warm glow. She returned the box and the badge to the desk drawer, and the doll to The Junk Basket. She put the basket lid back on, lowered the window blind, sat at the desk. She stayed in her room for a while longer, doing some of her homework. Then she went downstairs to watch TV, a soap she usually enjoyed. This evening it was images and words, none of it penetrating her mind. She was strangely calm, her feelings of fear and resentment and confusion blended into something that felt strong, a determination to put everything right at last.

When the soap was over, Mum called her into the kitchen for supper.

They sat in their usual places and ate, Mum making all the conversation, asking about Megan's day at school, Megan shrugging or nodding or giving one-word answers. Eventually Mum sighed and put down her knife and fork.

'I think we need to talk, Megan,' she said. 'Or rather, you do. You've got to stop being angry and move on, put the past behind you. We both have.'

'I'm not angry,' said Megan. 'I was, but I'm not any more.'

'Oh?' said Mum, surprised. 'Why is that? What's changed?'

At that moment Megan almost told her mum about the voodoo child, and what she intended to do. A dark eagerness was welling up inside her, and she wanted to share the certainty of her feelings. Surely Mum must want to get back at the woman who had taken Dad from them?

Then Megan realised Mum probably wouldn't believe a word of it, might even do something that would spoil the magic. No, this task was hers alone to perform. She would have to keep it to herself.

'I just think . . . everything's going to be all right, I suppose,' she said.

'I'm glad to hear it,' Mum said, smiling at her. 'So, does this mean you've finally come round to the idea that moving to a flat won't be so bad?'

'No, it doesn't,' Megan said. 'But then maybe we won't have to.'

'Oh, Megan,' Mum groaned. 'I've explained the reasons to you.'

'What if Dad came back though?' said Megan, trying not to give anything away, to control the words coming out of her mouth. 'I mean, I think we should wait a bit longer. In case he wants to, that is.'

Mum looked at Megan, her eyes full of sadness. 'It's not going to happen, love,' she said quietly. 'I didn't realise you thought it still might.'

'You don't know it won't. If Sarah wasn't around . . .'

'I do know, Megan. And I should have told you more; then perhaps you'd have understood earlier. But it was hard for me to talk about it.' Mum paused, looked down. 'The truth is,' she murmured, 'things hadn't been all that great between your father and me for a long time, even before Sarah came on the scene. I think we'd only stayed together because of you.'

The kitchen suddenly grew hazy, and Mum receded into the distance. Megan felt cold and shivery and sick, and she clenched her fists.

'What do you mean?' she said. Her voice sounded hollow to her, as if it wasn't her voice at all. 'Are you saying Sarah doesn't matter?'

'I'm sorry, love,' Mum said, looking up. 'She could vanish in a puff of smoke tomorrow and your father and I still wouldn't get back together . . .'

Mum's mouth kept moving, but Megan didn't hear another word.

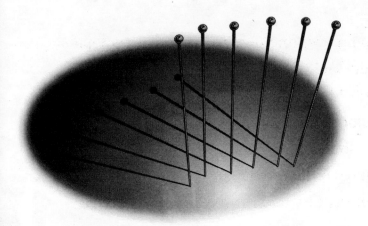

SIX: DIFFERENT LIGHT

Megan sat in bed, trying to read and failing. It was late, very late, the green numerals on the alarm clock showing that it was 11.58 p.m., but she just couldn't sleep. She had been brooding ever since Mum's revelation at supper, unable to stop going over and over in her mind what she had said. Of course it had been a shock, but Megan was beginning to think it actually explained a lot.

She had re-run her memories, like videos of the past, and saw her old life in a different light. She had thought about her parents' moodiness with each other and their arguments, and realised it was true: they hadn't been that happy together. Megan sighed. She closed her book and put it down on the bedside table. She shut her eyes, leaned her head against the pillow. So Sarah wasn't really to blame, she thought. Her parents would probably have split up eventually anyway. Which meant that maybe Mum was right. Maybe it was time to sell this house, put the past behind them, move on. All that voodoo stuff, thinking about hurting Sarah, even killing her . . . it was like a bad dream. Megan could hardly believe she'd actually felt that way.

That woman still deserves to die, hissed the voice. *Die, die, die . . .*

Megan had been expecting the voice, of course. But she immediately noticed there was something different about it now, an edge which hadn't been there before, a bitterness in that last word as it echoed inside her skull.

She opened her eyes, just caught the numerals on the clock changing to 12.00.

She looked beyond the clock, into the corner of the room where the shadows were thickest, and saw a pair of fiery yellow eyes burning in the darkness, staring at her. The voodoo child was beside The Junk Basket.

'But why?' Megan whispered. She could feel her heart thumping.

Why? said the voodoo child. *Because she shouldn't exist. Because this isn't the way it should be, should it? Dad should be here, with Mum, with . . .*

'Dad's not coming back though,' argued Megan. 'I don't think Mum even wants him back. So there's no point in killing Sarah. The old life is gone.'

Gone? the voodoo child wailed, the

harsh, shrill sound of the voice filling Megan's head, making her wince. *It can't be gone, gone, gone . . .*

'It is,' Megan whispered softly, almost inaudibly, and she suddenly felt as if she were letting it go, saying goodbye to it. 'Gone forever and ever.'

There was a brief silence, but a silence that prickled with menace. *Well then, we can't let them get away with it,* the voodoo child hissed.

'Who are you talking about?' Megan said, and then she understood, and she felt herself shiver with a new fear. 'Let them get away with what?'

The old life was a sham, a lie, the voodoo child muttered. *Mum and Dad deceived us, made us think we were happy, and then they ruined everything. So they must pay for what they did, what they're still doing.*

'But I don't want to make them pay for anything,' Megan whispered, wondering why the voodoo child had started to say 'we' and 'us'.

But we do, we do, hissed the voodoo child, the voice almost smug.

Then, with a jolt, Megan found herself standing in front of the wardrobe. The voodoo child flowed towards her till they were face to face, so close that they were almost touching. Megan realised that she and the voodoo child were the same size and height. She could see more features too; hair, eyebrows, a nose; a mouth more like a person's. A mouth like hers. In fact, Megan could see that the voodoo child was exactly like her – was a strange, dark, terrifying version of the self she saw in the mirror every day. Megan held her breath, and her heart seemed to stop. Everything fell into place.

Yes, that's right, Megan, said the voodoo child. *I am you and you are me. And I know what we really want. If we can't have the old life back, the one we thought we had . . . well, we just want to destroy, destroy, destroy . . .*

Megan let out her breath, but she couldn't speak. She looked down at her hands, saw that in one she was holding the Sarah doll, in the other a pin.

So first we start with . . . that woman, said the voodoo child. *And then we'll make dolls of Mum and Dad, and destroy them too. Hurt them, hurt them, hurt them; stick it in, stick it in, stick it in; do it, do it, do it . . .*

Megan felt the hand with the pin moving inexorably towards the doll. The voodoo child was a black cloud pressing on her, its outline blurring as it flowed into her, its darkness seeking the deeper pool of darkness that had always been inside her and from where it must have come.

Do it, do it, do it! the voodoo child hissed, and the pin moved closer and closer to the doll, its sharp point glinting. *Nobody cares about us, nobody!*

But there was another voice in Megan's head too, a small voice telling her that wasn't true. Mum had said she cared, hadn't she? And Dad had been trying to make it up to her in some way as well, even if he wasn't very good at doing it.

79

And what would happen if she did give in to this monster that she had unleashed? Megan knew it would be the end. The darkness inside her would fill the world, and she would never be happy again. Never. Never. And that's what she really wanted, Megan realised. Just to be happy.

Now the pin was almost touching the doll. Megan resisted its onward drive, resisted it with all her strength, but her hands and arms were shaking and she knew she couldn't hold it off much longer. She looked up, saw herself in the wardrobe mirror, and her mind nearly failed. She was the voodoo child now, an impossible creature of nightmare, fiery eyes burning with hate.

You can't do it, she hissed at herself.

I won't let you!

It's too late, she hissed back. *Stick it in, stick it in . . .*

Suddenly Megan knew that she could resist no more. There was only one thing she could do, only one thing that might still save her.

She concentrated on the hand holding the doll, willed her thumb to move, to lie across the Sarah doll's chest. But the pin was getting closer and closer and closer, and her thumb wouldn't budge. Then suddenly her thumb twitched and slipped into place . . . just in time for her other hand to plunge the pin into it.

She felt the sharp point prick her skin, felt the realness of the pain, and she cried out and dropped both the doll and the pin to the floor.

Megan closed her eyes and concentrated on the darkness inside her.

She pushed it down, down, down into that pool, until it was all in there. Then she squeezed the pool itself, squeezing and squeezing it into a ball of blackness, and pushed it deeper and deeper and deeper until it disappeared. She heard a final hissing, a final wailed *Noooooooooo* . . . and then nothing.

She waited for a moment, hardly daring to believe that she had succeeded.

Then she took a deep breath and slowly opened her eyes once more.

Megan looked in the wardrobe mirror. She was relieved to see that it was herself she was looking at, not a creature of darkness, just an ordinary, dark-haired girl wearing pyjamas, standing in her room, with the golden glow of the bedside lamp keeping the shadows penned in the corners. Megan listened, but all she could hear was silence and her own quick breathing.

Her eyes briefly flashed yellow, then faded to their normal green.

She sat on the bed and looked down at her thumb, at the tiny globe of bright red blood that stood out from the skin. She put her mouth to it, sucked the blood away, its salty, iron taste lingering on her tongue. Megan could see the spot where the point of the pin had entered, felt a soreness there. And she wondered if that was it, if the voodoo child was gone forever and

they were safe . . . She wasn't worried though. She knew she would be able to deal with it if it ever happened again, that she would know what to do. But now she was tired, so tired, and she had to rest. She slid into bed, falling asleep as soon as her head touched the pillow . . .

The next thing she knew it was morning, daylight seeping round the blind. Megan sat up. She hadn't had any dreams. She felt OK. No, better than OK – she felt normal, like her old self. She jumped out of bed, and then she saw the doll and the pin, lying where she had dropped them the night before. Megan picked them up, put them on the desk.

Just an old doll and a pin, she thought. That's all they were.

She got washed and dressed, went downstairs for breakfast, saw that Mum was already in the garden, raking leaves again. Megan went outside to join her. The air was cold, and the sky was dark and filled with big, grey clouds.

'You're up bright and early for a Saturday,' said Mum. 'Have you got plans for today? I thought you weren't seeing your dad till tomorrow.'

'I thought I might start sorting out my stuff,' Megan said, and shrugged. 'Maybe get rid of some old things. I'll need to . . . if we're going to move.'

Mum smiled and came over to her. She cupped her daughter's cheek with her hand and kissed her softly, and Megan leaned into her mother's warmth.

The two of them stood together for a moment, holding on to each other.

'That's a good idea, love,' said Mum at last. 'I've got some sorting out of my own to do, so I'll help you too, if you like. But only on one condition.'

'Don't tell me,' said Megan. 'You want me to put the kettle on.'

'Cheeky,' said Mum, ruffling her hair. 'But you've got it in one.'

Megan's smile was like the sun rising, chasing away the night.

DEADLY GAME

CONTENTS

ONE: VOICES CALLING

Jake is sitting on an old wooden bench in the small back garden of the holiday cottage, reading one of his comics for the umpteenth time, keeping his head down to shield his eyes from the bright morning sunshine. Keeping his head down in another way too. With a bit of luck Mum and Dad and Hannah might leave him alone, and that would suit him just fine.

But soon he can hear noises in the cottage, doors being opened and closed, footsteps, his parents' voices calling, calling. The words are muffled, yet Jake can make them out – 'Jake! Jake, where are you?' He doesn't answer. The bench is hard to see from the bedrooms and the kitchen window. Even so, Jake hunches his shoulders, concentrates more intently on his comic.

Then the back door opens and Dad appears. 'So that's where you've been hiding,' Dad says. 'Come on, we're going out.'

'I don't want to go out,' Jake mutters.

'I'm happy where I am.'

'No choice I'm afraid, pal. We're all in this together. It'll be fun, you'll see.'

Jake raises an eyebrow, gives his father a you-must-be-joking look. But he knows there's not much point in arguing, and closes his comic with a deep sigh. 'That's my boy!' says Dad, smiling at him, and they go inside.

Mum and Hannah are in the hall, Hannah sucking her thumb while Mum fusses over her, making sure she has plenty of suncream on any exposed skin, insisting she wears her hat.

Jake thinks how alike they are, both slim redheads with freckly skin and green eyes. Dad is tall, fair-haired and blue-eyed, and everyone says Jake looks like him, although Jake doesn't agree.

Jake isn't tall for a twelve year old, and his hair is muddy brown, his eyes greeny-grey. He's wearing a red T-shirt and blue jeans, Hannah a yellow dress and white shoes, and their parents are in casual holiday clothes and trainers. Jake notices that Mum doesn't mention suncream or a hat to him.

Hannah takes her thumb from her mouth, smiles at Jake uncertainly.

'We're going to see the stones, Jake,' she says. 'The magic stones.'

Jake ignores her. 'What's happening then?' he says, glancing from Dad to Mum. Hannah's smile fades, and she slips her thumb in her mouth again.

'I wish you wouldn't do that, Jake,'

Mum says, frowning at him.

'Do what?' he says, although he knows perfectly well what she means.

'Treat your sister as if she doesn't exist. I've told you ...'

'We're off to visit the local ancient monument,' Dad says hurriedly, 'which is even older than me, amazingly enough. Right, everybody ready?'

Jake shrugs. Mum shakes her head, and they all go out to the people carrier, Dad taking the driver's seat, Mum next to him, Hannah and Jake in the rear. They drive through the village and turn on to the main road that brought them from the city a few days ago. Jake still has his comic, and he buries his nose in it, trying not to listen as Dad chatters about where they're headed, a stone circle like Stonehenge. Mum doesn't speak, and Jake can tell she's still cross. But then she's always cross with him at the moment.

He looks out of his window at the fields whizzing past, a line of low hills beyond them, a huge, fluffy white cloud hanging motionless in an otherwise clear blue sky. He's glad Dad cut Mum off before she could build up a head of steam. Not that she needs to give him the lecture any

more. Jake knows it by heart – *be nice to Hannah, there's no reason to be horrible to her, she's had enough problems without you adding to them, blah blah blah.* Mind you, Dad could give the same lecture too. He gets just as cross, although lately he's been playing Mr Nice Guy, the family peacemaker.

'You two OK in the back?' says Dad, glancing at them in the rear-view mirror. 'We'll be there soon. It's only a couple of miles from the village.'

'There are *three* of us in the back,' says Hannah in the mock-sulky tone Jake hates. 'And Mr James wants to know where we're having lunch.'

Oh no, not Mr James, thinks Jake. He's been hoping there might be some escape from Hannah's imaginary friend on holiday. At home it's really been getting out of hand, Hannah insisting Mum and Dad set a place for Mr James at every meal, even leave room for him on the sofa when they're watching TV. And to Jake's disgust Mum and Dad have been going along with it.

'You can tell Mr James we've brought a picnic,' says Mum, smiling at her. 'We'll eat it at the stone circle, after we've had a look at everything.'

'Did you hear that, Mr James?' says Hannah, speaking to the empty space between her and her brother. 'A picnic! We can play games as well. I –'

'Isn't she a bit old to have an imaginary friend?' Jake mutters, interrupting her. 'I mean, she's nearly eight. If you ask me it's all a bit creepy.'

'Nobody *was* asking you, Jake,' says Mum, scowling at him, 'and if you've got nothing nice to say about your sister, don't say anything.'

She turns to face forward, and Jake sticks his tongue out at her. Dad spots him in the rear-view mirror and frowns, but Jake doesn't care. He glances at Hannah. Her thumb is planted firmly in her mouth. She's staring at him, and Jake can see in

her eyes that she's not very happy either. Good, he thinks.

A few moments later they pass a sign that tells them they've arrived. They leave the main road and go down a track between hawthorn hedges, finally emerging in a car park which looks pretty full. But Dad finds a space, and they stop.

Jake sees that on the far side of the car park there's a picnic area with a few tables and benches, and beyond them, a dense, shadow-filled grove of trees. On the near side is a small steel and glass building with another sign, one that says *VISITOR CENTRE*. And directly in front of them is a grassy hill, the last and lowest of those Jake had seen from the car. On it stand the ancient stones, dark and massive in the morning sun.

HUMAN SACRIFICES

They get out the car, but to Jake's surprise they don't head straight up the hill. Then he sees that the stones are fenced off, and realises that to reach them you have to pass through the Visitor Centre, which seems very busy. They go in and queue at the ticket desk, where they're served at last by an elderly lady who chats with Mum and Dad and coos soppily over Hannah.

Jake doesn't want to hear any of it, and wanders off on his own.

The building is deceptive, its interior larger than it seems from outside. There are no inner walls. The exhibits and displays are in glass cases or on moveable partitions, and red arrows painted on the floor show you which way to go. At the rear is a cluster of computer terminals, and beyond them a row of tall windows, a glass door in the centre of it leading to the stone circle. Jake follows the arrows, his trainers squeaking faintly on the polished floor, the voices of the people around him muted in the cavernous space.

After a while he reaches the computers. He's not that interested, but he touches an icon on a screen. A picture appears, an artist's impression of a ceremony – a child stretched out on a great stone at the centre of the circle, a man in a dark cloak standing there with his arms raised, a crowd surrounding them. Jake leans forward to examine the man more closely. Is that a knife in one of his hands? The displays had explained that the circle was probably some kind of temple, a place where people had gathered to watch priests performing rituals. They must have gone in for human sacrifices too …

'Jake! Come on, Jake, we're waiting for you!'

Jake looks round. Mum is standing in the open doorway, silhouetted by the sunlight beyond, her face in shadow. Jake slowly walks over to her. Dad and Hannah are outside, and already some distance along the path that leads from the Visitor

Centre to the stone circle. They pause and look back.

'You two carry on ahead,' Mum calls out. 'We'll catch you up!'

Dad waves, then turns and puts an arm around Hannah's shoulders, leaning over her protectively. They resume their climb, and Mum sets off along the path as well. Jake trails after her, a step or two behind, squinting in the sunlight, convinced he's about to get the same old lecture. But he's wrong.

'Listen, Jake,' Mum says. 'If I could change the past, I would. I know things were difficult because of Hannah's illness, and I'm sorry if you felt left out sometimes.' Jake glances at her, doesn't speak. 'I also know lots of brothers and sisters don't get on. But the way you've been acting recently, well ...' Mum stops, Jake almost bumping into her. 'Can't you be a bit nicer?' she says, squeezing his shoulder. 'To us, and to Hannah. Life's too short for all this ...' She pauses, but he stays silent. 'Think about it, OK?' she says quietly. Then she smiles at him, turns round, walks on up the path.

Jake watches her go, anger flooding through him. It's so easy for her to say those things. A few words, a smile, and suddenly he's supposed to start behaving like the perfect son and brother, is he? Well, maybe he would – if they acted like proper parents to him. He needs some kind of proof that Hannah's not their favourite, that *he* matters to them as much as she does. But they never pay him any attention – except when he's horrible to her.

Which is why he does it, of course, although sometimes he feels a little guilty about his behaviour, a little worried about the kind of person he's becoming. But he's not going to give in to them. Not in a million years. Why should he? *He* didn't bring Hannah into the world. Mum and Dad did …

He sets off again, trudging up the path in the warm sunshine, his anger hot inside him. The sky is still a brilliant blue; that big, fluffy white cloud moving now, its shadow crossing the side of the hill and sliding up towards the crest, like a great beast swimming through the sea, Jake thinks. He and the shadow reach the entrance to the circle together, and darkness briefly passes over him, a breath of wind ruffling his hair and tugging at his T-shirt.

The entrance is a giant's doorway – two enormous, dark-grey upright stones, at least five metres tall and a couple wide, a third of equal size laid across their tops. Jake stops and looks in. The rest of the circle is made up of similar stones arranged in the same way, although some have fallen and left large gaps. Lots of people are wandering around, little children running and laughing. Jake sees that there's also an inner ring of smaller stones, and glimpses three familiar figures moving within it. His parents and Hannah.

He walks on through the entrance and instantly feels a change in the air, the skin on his face and bare arms tingling, a strange, rather unpleasant sensation. Jake tries to ignore it, thinking it must be to do with the heat, the sun now being directly overhead. But he can't, especially as the feeling grows more powerful with every step he takes deeper into the circle.

He comes to the inner ring, goes inside. And there at the very centre is the stone he saw on the computer. It's almost circular, a metre high and two metres across, and its rough, slightly concave surface is so dark it seems to suck in the sunlight. The tingle in Jake's skin becomes a shudder, and he finds himself thinking there's something about this place he doesn't like.

Dad is kneeling in front of the stone. Mum has her arm round Hannah's shoulders.

'The Heart Stone,' Dad reads from a plaque set in the ground. 'Probably the original altar ... There's a legend that if you touch it when you make a wish, your wish will come true. Oh, there you are, Jake.'

Mum and Hannah look round at Jake, then briefly at each other.

'Just in time!' says Mum. 'Your sister wants me to play hide and seek with her, but I can't run around in this heat. How about you, Jake?'

'Yes, Jake,' says Hannah. 'Will you play with me? Please?'

There is a moment of silence and stillness. Jake looks at his sister, at his parents hanging on his answer. He feels the immensity of the sky above, the brooding presence of the stones around them. A voice deep inside him tries to make itself heard. But his anger is too dark, too bitter, too strong.

'No thanks,' he says. 'I don't play stupid baby games.'

Mum and Dad both scowl and Hannah's face crumbles.

'You're *so* horrible, Jake!' she sobs, and turns away from him. She reaches out to touch the Heart Stone, mumbles something Jake can't hear.

Suddenly, white light explodes in his head and he is falling, falling …

SOUNDLESS SCREAM

After a time Jake realises his eyes are closed and he opens them.

He stares up at pale, ragged clouds streaming across a dark, starless sky, occasional lightning flashes giving them a brief inner glow. Dull, distant rumbles seem to be making the ground tremble beneath him. The ground ... he's lying on the ground. He can feel a pebble pressing painfully into a shoulder blade, grass tickling the soft skin on the inside of a forearm.

He gets to his feet and looks around. There's light coming from somewhere, but it's poor, and shapes are blurred, colours reduced to shades of grey. Jake can see he's alone in the inner ring of the stone circle though. In exactly the same spot he remembers being, in fact, before ...

Before what? Did he pass out? It hadn't felt like that. He casts his mind back, trying to remember the sequence of events. Hannah said something, and he felt as if he were falling, as if a hole had opened beneath him and he'd tumbled into it. Jake looks down at himself. He seems OK. No bones broken, no cuts or bruises. And there are no holes nearby, nothing to explain what happened, where his parents and Hannah might have gone.

Another, brighter flash lights the clouds and there's a deeper rumble, one that vibrates in his bones. A cold gust of wind buffets him and Jake begins to feel afraid. Perhaps a war has started, he thinks. Perhaps the white light was a nuclear explosion; perhaps the falling sensation was caused by a blast; perhaps the flashes and rumbles are more bombs going off; perhaps the clouds are the smoke of burning cities. Perhaps his parents and Hannah and everyone else in the world are dead and he's the last person left alive ...

Jake takes a deep breath, lets it out, forces himself to calm down. There must be a simpler explanation. Then another thought pops into his mind and he feels angry again. Whatever happened, Mum and Dad have obviously run away with their precious Hannah – abandoning *him* to his fate. But that's OK, Jake decides. He can take care of himself. And he'll start by getting out of this creepy place and finding someone who can tell him what's going on.

He strides down the path, away from the Heart Stone and out of the inner ring. There's nobody in the circle, so he goes out the way he came in. He breaks into a jog, heads for the Visitor Centre. The rear door is open, and he steps inside. It's as deserted as the circle, no lights on, the cavernous interior thick with shadows. Jake suddenly feels a surge of fear again, and he pauses for an instant just inside the door, scalp crawling, heart pounding. Then he frowns, tells himself not to be so stupid, makes for the ticket desk.

An enormous flash in the sky outside momentarily floods the entire building with light. The darkness quickly returns, but the brief illumination has allowed Jake to glimpse something that stops him in his tracks.

The picture in the nearest display looks like … but it can't be!

There are more flashes, and Jake soon sees that it's exactly what he thought – a photograph of his family; Mum and Dad and Hannah and him. A posed shot which seems to have been taken at their cottage that very morning, before they'd set out for the stone circle. But he doesn't remember posing for a picture. Who could have taken it, anyway? More importantly, what is it doing here? Suddenly Jake feels the skin on the back of his neck prickling, and he has an irresistible urge to look over his shoulder …

The computers are glowing, each terminal showing the same picture as the display, his family repeated over and over again on every screen.

Jake's heart is hammering now. He struggles to keep a grip, to stay calm. He turns round, walks on. He notices the red arrows on the floor are glowing too, and that they're pointing in the opposite direction to the way they were earlier. He tries not to think about it, or look at the displays he passes. But each flash outside reveals more pictures of his family, different ones.

Mum and Dad with Jake aged about five, all of them smiling, Mum pregnant; baby Hannah in an incubator, Mum and Dad looking worried; Hannah in hospital for yet another operation to sort out the problem with her kidney; Jake with Nan

and Grandad, staying at their house; Mum and Dad with Hannah at home, Jake in the background looking uncertain; Hannah, a toddler, Jake playing with her; Hannah in hospital again; Hannah at home, Mum fussing over her, Jake scowling; Jake pushing an older Hannah away, Dad shouting, Jake shouting at him, Jake being told off by Mum,

Jake sulking, Jake being horrible to Hannah again, and again, and again ...

He stands in front of the last display, scared and horrified and amazed in equal measure. Suddenly the back of his neck prickles once more. He slowly looks round and another flash of lightning reveals the elderly lady in her place behind the ticket desk. But now her face is distorted, her eyes slits of hate, her mouth impossibly wide in a soundless scream, her hair streaming behind her. She moves her hand up in slow motion and points ... at him.

Jake backs away from her, terrified and whimpering. Then he flees, the elderly lady's finger moving to keep pace with him as he runs past her. He slams into the front door, pushes it open, shoots out

into the car park.

That's empty too, every single car that was parked there gone, except for one – their people carrier. It's still in the same spot, looking small and forlorn in the middle of all that open space. Jake pauses, confused, desperately looking round for his family, for anyone. Then he catches sight of a figure walking towards the people carrier – it's Dad! Jake is filled with relief, even though he's angry with his parents, and he runs across the tarmac. He comes up to Dad, slows down, walks along beside him.

'Dad, what's going on?' he gabbles breathlessly. 'Why did you and Mum leave me in the circle? I thought you were ... and something really weird happened in the Visitor Centre, there are these pictures of us, and that lady, she's, she's ...' Jake pauses, his anger flaring. He realises that Dad is taking absolutely no notice, hasn't even looked at him, not once. 'What is this, the silent treatment?' Jake snaps. 'Hello? Dad?' he says, raising his voice.

But Dad still says nothing, still doesn't look at him. He studies Dad's face. Dad is smiling, and now Jake feels more confused, more frightened than ever. It's as if Dad can't see or hear him, as if he's become invisible … Just then they reach the people carrier and Dad opens the boot. He lifts out the picnic box, closes the boot again, bleeps it locked. He turns and starts walking back in the same direction, goes past Jake. Jake follows him.

'Dad?' Jake says, almost pleading. He stops after a few steps, watches Dad heading towards the picnic area, hears him whistling a jaunty tune.

Jake glances beyond him – and what he sees makes his blood freeze.

DEAD EYES

Three people are sitting at one of the picnic tables, waiting for Dad – Mum, Hannah, and a boy of his own age Jake has never seen before, although he seems familiar. He's staring at Jake across the car park, his face hard, unsmiling. Then the boy turns to Mum, laughs at something she's saying, says something in reply that makes her laugh, although Hannah doesn't.

Jake watches Dad take the picnic box over to them. The boy helps Mum and Dad unpack it and passes a carton of juice to Hannah, just as if he were one of the family. Jake has the strangest feeling as he looks on. Anyone who didn't know them would probably think the boy was Mum and Dad's son, and Hannah's brother. But he's not, Jake tells himself, his anger flooding back, swamping the uneasiness he'd felt at Dad's behaviour. Jake decides this must be a practical joke, some elaborate scheme devised by his parents to make him see the error of his ways. Yes, that's it – those pictures in the Visitor Centre, the elderly lady, it's all a performance for his benefit ...

Well, it's not very funny, Jake thinks. In fact it's cruel, practically child abuse, and he marches across the empty car park to give his parents a piece of his mind. He stops near the picnic table, stands there seething with anger, waits for Mum and Dad to look at him, to acknowledge his presence. But they don't. They carry on with what they're doing as if he wasn't there.

'Hello? Jake calling parents,' he says. There's no reaction. Mum and Dad continue to pass things to Hannah, who's not looking at Jake, and to the boy. He glances at Jake once or twice, but mostly keeps his attention on Mum and Dad.

'Hey!' says Jake, more loudly, standing in his parents' sight line. 'Very funny, Mum and Dad. I know you can see me ...'

He waves both hands at them. Nothing. Mum and Dad and the boy chat and laugh in the way happy families do when they're having a picnic. It's too much for Jake. Doubt fills his mind, and suddenly he feels that he's trapped in a nightmare. His anger and fear boil up inside him, and he opens his mouth to yell and scream …

'I wouldn't do that if I were you,' says the boy, his voice quiet but firm.

Jake whips round, glares across the table. The boy meets his gaze calmly. Jake sees now that he's much the same size as him, and wearing the same kind of T-shirt as he is, although the boy's is blue. 'What business is it of yours what I do?' Jake snaps. 'And who the hell are you, anyway?'

'Why, Jake,' says the boy, a mocking smile playing round his lips. 'I'm surprised you haven't guessed. You must be even more of a moron than I took you for. Oh well … shall I tell him, Hannah, or will you?' Jake catches Hannah staring at him, a strange, almost fearful expression on her face. But all Jake can think is that she can see him … 'OK, I'll do it then,' says the boy, his voice breaking into Jake's thoughts. 'I'm afraid there's no easy way to put this, Jake, so I'll just have to be brutal. I'm your replacement.'

'My … replacement?' says Jake. 'What are you talking about?'

'I'm in and you're out,' says the boy, shrugging. 'I'm Mum and Dad's son now, and Hannah's big brother, and you're not any more. That's about as simple as I can make it. I've even got your comic,' he says, pulling it from his back pocket and tossing it on the table. 'Although I must say I'm not very impressed by your taste in reading matter ... OK, I think that covers everything. I suggest you disappear and let us get on with our picnic ...'

'Whoa there!' says Jake. 'You're having me on, aren't you?'

The boy sighs, shakes his head. 'No, Jake, I'm not,' he says. 'But I can see you won't get this until I lay the whole thing out for you. Remember when Hannah asked you to play hide and seek with her in the circle and you said no? That upset her, so she wished that her imaginary friend could be her brother instead of you. And because she touched the Heart Stone at the same time, her wish came true. I'm right, aren't I, Hannah?' Hannah looks up from her paper plate, glances at him and at Jake. She nods, looks down at her plate again. 'So zap, pow, alakazam …' says the boy, 'here I am.'

'That's crazy,' Jake murmurs, but there's an unsettling quality about the boy's confidence. Jake studies him closely for the first time and realises he seems familiar because there's a strong family

resemblance between them. In fact, they could easily be taken for brothers. Except for one thing. The boy's eyes aren't blue like Dad's, or green like Mum's and Hannah's, or even greeny-grey like Jake's. His eyes are cold, flat, colourless. Dead eyes, Jake thinks. 'So you're telling me you're Mr James, and that you've magically been made into a real person?' Jake says, trying to keep his voice steady, and failing. 'It's like something from a fairy tale. It can't happen.'

'Oh, but it has, Jake,' says the boy. 'And it's just plain James, actually. Hannah and I decided to drop the Mr, didn't we, sis?' Hannah says nothing, slips her thumb into her mouth. 'I know it's hard to believe, Jake. But you should bear in mind there's a lot of power in an ancient site like this. Come on, accept it. What other explanation could there be, anyway? Take a peep at yourself if you want more proof. There's more light here to see by.'

Jake does as he's told, and his heart seems to stop when he realises that his T-shirt, his jeans, his trainers are still grey, even in better light – material, stitching, buttons, leather, laces, everything. Exactly the same shade of grey.

'Oh dear, Jake,' says the boy. 'You look as though you've seen a ghost.'

LOST SOULS

Jake tries to speak, but no words come out. He looks up, allows the utter weirdness of his surroundings to sink in. The eerie light that fills the picnic area though the sky is dark, his parents behaving as if nothing strange were happening, the boy – or rather *James* – watching him with his dead eyes.

This isn't a practical joke or an elaborate hoax, Jake thinks. It's not a hallucination, either, not a dream or a nightmare. It's terrifyingly real.

'Ah, I do believe we're reading from the same page at last,' says James. 'Is there anything else you'd like to know? Any details I can fill in for you?'

'What's happened to me?' says Jake. 'Why are my clothes all grey?'

'That's because you're in a different world,' says James. 'Or perhaps I should call it a different dimension. Whatever, it's where imaginary friends lead their poor, thin, sad existences. A place with no life, and no colour.'

'But you're not all grey …' says Jake. He glances at his sister. She's following the conversation, her eyes flicking between the two boys. 'Wait a minute – how come you and Hannah can see me but Mum and Dad can't? And why aren't they taking any notice of you and what you're saying?'

'You really are a bit slow on the uptake, Jake, aren't you?' says James. 'Look, *you're* the imaginary friend now, OK?' He talks slowly, as if he's speaking to a toddler, Jake realises. And not a very bright toddler at that, either. 'So Hannah can see you, of course, and I can too. But Mum and Dad can't because they're grown-ups, and everybody knows that grown-ups don't have imaginary friends. And they don't take much notice of us kids when they think we're playing, especially if we're not bothering them.'

James leans back and folds his arms, a smug expression on his face, challenging Jake to disagree, to prove him wrong. But Jake isn't going to.

'OK, I believe you,' Jake murmurs. 'It's

seriously weird, but not much more than the idea of a wish actually coming true. 'So how long will it be before things return to normal? Before I get out of this … dimension?'

'I wouldn't hold your breath,' says James. 'I think you should probably plan on a fairly lengthy stay. Actually, the word *forever* comes to mind.'

A chill runs down Jake's spine, and he swallows, his throat tight.

'Forever?' he asks, his voice sounding very small. There's a bright flash in the sky above, a deep, distant rumble. 'But what am I supposed to do?'

'Do?' says James. He gets up, walks round the table and past Hannah, his face suddenly hard and unsmiling again. He stands in front of Jake. 'As an imaginary friend you don't *do* anything. Oh, you hang around, you listen and sympathise and, finally, when the time comes, when Hannah grows out of the imaginary friend stage and doesn't need you any more ...' He pauses, raises a hand, flutters his fingers and makes a slow, falling gesture. He smiles, his dead eyes fixed on Jake's. 'Well then, you simply fade away.'

'I don't understand,' says Jake. 'Do you mean I'm going ... to die?'

'Oh no,' says James. 'It's far worse than that. Once you lose your reason for being, you become one of the lost souls, forever trapped in nothingness. There are a few over there in the trees, Jake. Take a look at your future.'

Jake turns and peers at the glade behind the picnic area. At first all he can make out is dense shadow, dark trunks, branches with stiff black leaves that rattle in a brief gust of wind. Then he begins to make out dim, grey shapes flitting and swooping between the trees. He hears them hissing, whispering, sees them gathering at the edge of the glade, watching him, waiting ...

Jake catches his breath, whimpers again, steps backwards.

'I'm not going to end up in there,' he mutters. 'Not like *them*.'

'You don't have a lot of choice,' says James. 'You're …'

'Just be quïet, will you?' says Jake, his anger flaring inside him once more. He glimpses Hannah staring at him from behind James, and pushes past him, walking round the table to stand over her. 'So I've got you to thank for this, have I?' he says. Hannah sucks her thumb harder, lowers her head and looks up at him, her eyes wide. 'For being trapped here forever, for fading away? Well, cheers, Hannah, that's terrific. I suppose I should have known you'd manage to get rid of me

56

eventually. Some sister *you* are.'

Hannah winces at every word, then lowers her eyes and looks away.

'Temper, temper,' says James. 'You really should try to develop more self-control, Jake. It might help you to avoid saying things you'll regret.'

'*Now* what are you talking about?' Jake glares at him.

'Perhaps I should have told you earlier,' says James. 'Actually, there *is* a way out of all this. But it's the only way, and I have a feeling you might just have blown it.' He pauses, a smile on his face. Jake waits, his mouth dry, his heart pounding, a pulse beating like a drum in his head. 'It's rather simple,' says James. 'Hannah made the wish. So Hannah can unmake it too.'

James turns to her. 'Although you probably don't want to now, do you, sis?'

Hannah looks up at Jake again – and suddenly he feels sick …

SIX

TURNING POINT

Jake stands there, his stomach churning, his mind in a whirl. He feels he should say something, take back what he said to Hannah, but he doesn't know where to start. He looks at her, opens his mouth, closes it again.

'I'm impressed, Jake,' says James. 'What a terrific impersonation of a fish! Or maybe you're just lost for words … I would be, if I were you.'

Jake grits his teeth, clenches his fists. He's had enough of being taunted by this imposter. 'Well, you're not me,' he says, taking a couple of steps towards the other boy. Jake gives him his hardest, meanest playground stare. 'And you're not taking *my* place in *my* family,' he adds. 'Got that?'

'Oooh,' says James. 'I'm really scared … er, not. But I tell you what. I'll give you a chance. Hannah can choose which of us she wants as her brother, OK? We'll each put our case, then Hannah can decide between us, and the loser has to accept defeat. You'll go along with that, won't you, Hannah?'

Hannah looks at Jake, then back at James. She nods, slipping her thumb in her mouth immediately afterwards. James turns to Jake and smirks at him.

'So … how about it, Jake?' he says. 'You don't have much to lose.'

Jake's stomach twists, and his mouth fills with the warm, bitter taste of fear. He knows this is the turning point, that his whole life is held in the balance at this moment. He looks at Mum and Dad. They're still sitting at the table, eating and talking quietly to each other, oblivious to what's happening. What did Dad say about their outing today? That it would be fun ... Well, you were wrong, Dad, Jake thinks. He takes a deep breath and turns to face James.

'OK, it's a deal,' he says, with far more confidence than he feels.

'Right, let's give ourselves some room,' says James. He strides away from the picnic area, gesturing to Hannah to follow him, which she does, giving Jake a strange backward glance he can't interpret, her eyes briefly locking on his. Jake follows, stops when James and Hannah do, the three of them forming a rough triangle, Hannah at the apex, James and Jake at either ends of the base. 'Well, here we are, all nicely in position,' says James. 'I suppose we should toss a coin to see who goes first. Have you got a coin, Jake?'

'I ... I don't think so,' says Jake, patting the pockets of his jeans.

'I'll go first then,' says James. He turns to Hannah, squares his shoulders, gathers himself like an actor preparing to give an important speech in a play.

'Hannah,' he says, smiling, drawing out her name, his voice caressing it, 'we haven't known each other long, not properly, anyway. But you know I've always been there for you, and I think you've realised now that I'm a much better prospect as a big brother than Jake … who's a total waste of space.'

'Hey, that's not fair,' Jake yells. 'You're just running me down!'

'All's fair in love and families, Jakey boy,' James snaps. 'And I'm only telling the truth. You *are* a total waste of space. You've been horrible to Hannah since the day she was born, and mean to Mum and Dad. You're eaten up inside with jealousy, you're vicious and vile and selfish …'

Jake listens as James lists his bad qualities, all the bad things he's done, the relentless voice finding the part of him that feels guilty, oh so guilty. Jake looks up at the clouds streaming across the dark sky, sees the flashes, hears the rumbles, and suddenly his mind isn't in a whirl any more. His anger disappears and he's convinced that everything James says is right. Of course Mum and Dad were worried about Hannah. She'd nearly died, for God's sake! But what had *he* done? Made their lives miserable with his constant demands for attention. So what kind of person behaves like that? The kind of person who doesn't deserve to be part of a good family ...

'OK, OK,' Jake says at last, looking

down, stopping James in mid-rant. 'I've heard enough,' he whispers. 'More than enough. You win ...'

'Really?' says James. 'You mean you don't you want to try and put your case?' Jake shakes his head. 'You're absolutely *sure*?' Jake nods.

James closes his eyes, tips his head back for a second, breathes deeply.

'Yes ...!' he hisses, then smiles and opens his eyes. Jake can see they're not flat and colourless any more. They're shiny, black and glinting with triumph.

'Good call, Jake,' James says after a moment. 'Now why don't you just run along? You said yourself that Hannah's too old for an imaginary friend, so you're not needed any more. I feel a clean break would be best, don't you?

'I'm going,' says Jake. He looks at the trees, sees the grey shapes waiting. He shivers, but his mind is made up. 'Is it OK if I say goodbye though?'

'Be my guest,' says James. 'But don't drag it out.'

Hannah hasn't moved. Jake starts walking towards her, then stops. Her little face is sad and Jake can feel his eyes prickling. 'I'm sorry, Hannah. For everything. I should have been nicer to you. You'll be much happier without me around. Take care of yourself, OK?' Jake isn't sure, but he thinks Hannah's bottom lip is trembling. He quickly turns away, heads for the picnic area, stands in front of Mum and Dad. 'I should have been a

better son to you too,' he whispers, a tear spilling on to his cheek. 'I'm sorry ...'

Mum and Dad are talking quietly, but suddenly they both go very still.

They turn slowly to face him. They're squinting, peering like people trying to see through a mist. 'Jake ... is that you?' Mum says hesitantly, and now Jake is certain they've heard him, that they can see him too. But then the moment passes and they look away as if he's become invisible again.

'Come on, Jakey boy, hurry up,' snarls James. 'Just go, will you?'

Jake glares at him, new questions already forming on his lips, his anger welling up inside him again. But then something else surprising happens.

Hannah speaks.

DEADLY GAME

'I don't want Jake to go,' she says, her small, pure voice carrying clearly across the empty car park. Jake looks at his little sister in her yellow dress, immense darkness above and beyond her, and he realises how tiny and vulnerable she is.

But there's determination in her face too, her eyes fierce with it. 'He can't go,' she says. 'I haven't done the choosing yet.'

'But you don't need to,' says James. 'Jake's already done it for you ...'

'That doesn't matter,' Hannah says firmly. 'You said *I* had to do it.'

'OK then, sweetheart,' James says, briefly giving her a cold smile. 'Let's hear your big decision. I hope you've been thinking about it *very* hard.'

'I have,' says Hannah. 'I choose ... Jake to be my brother.' A huge flash fills the sky, followed by an enormous rumble.

Hannah runs to Jake and looks up into his eyes. 'I'm sorry too, Jake,' she says, the words tumbling from her. 'But you were horrible, and I made the wish and you fell over and Mr James came and I thought he was nice, but he isn't, he's different and he's creepy and more horrible than you ever were, and I don't like him, and then you said you were sorry so I knew you were nice, but I always did ...'

'It's OK, Hannah,' Jake says. 'You've got nothing to be sorry for.' He draws her close, his guilt deepening. He should have realised she'd been terrified by the consequences of her wish ... and suddenly he knows what else he wants to say. 'It's going to be different from now on, Hannah, I promise,' he whispers. '*I'm* going to be different. I'll look after you. All you have to do is unmake your wish, then everything will be all right ...'

'Ah, how sweet,' says a voice. Jake looks

round. James is watching them, his smile even colder than before. 'A touching scene … and a classic happy ending to your story,' he says. 'It's such a pity I'll have to spoil it.'

'You leave us alone,' says Jake, scowling at the other boy. 'We made a deal, remember? Hannah's chosen me, and you have to accept defeat.'

James laughs at him. 'You're crazy if you think I'm going back to being Mr James,' he says. 'Grey isn't my colour, and I'm far too young to fade away. I'm very disappointed in you, Hannah. This could all have been so easy. Now I suppose I'll just have to switch to Plan B, unluckily for you …'

'We're not listening,' says Jake. 'Come

on, Hannah, let's go.'

'Stop right there,' James says, his voice suddenly harsh and menacing. 'You two aren't going anywhere. Plan B involves me killing Hannah, for obvious reasons.' Jake feels Hannah breathe in sharply, her small body trembling, and he grips her shoulder. 'But I'm afraid I'm going to have to kill you first, Jake. Mum and Dad are very attached to you. They were both so moved by your farewell speech I thought for a second they might pull you back into the real world. Which means I can't take the risk of you being left hanging around after I've disposed of Hannah, not even as a lost soul ...'

So they do love me, Jake realises. James has just given him something he's wanted for a long time, real proof that Mum and Dad do care about him. All his anger and resentment fade away and he feels oddly calm. Then Hannah squeezes his hand, looks up at him and he focuses on James once more.

'Take your best shot, pal,' Jake says, pushing Hannah behind him. 'I can handle you, no problem.' He's sure he could beat James in a straight fight. They're the same size, after all. Or at least they were ...

'I don't think so,' says James, and grins at them. He starts to grow, and soon doubles in size, his arms and shoulders rippling with muscle, his hands huge. He looms over them, his face terrifying, evil. Hannah screams, and Jake gasps.

'But let's make this fun, shall we?' says James. 'You said you don't play stupid baby games, Jake. Well, let's play a deadly game of hide and seek. You run off and hide while I count to ten. One, two, three ...'

Jake turns and flees, grabbing Hannah's hand and pulling her with him, making for the Visitor Centre. They go in, and Jake shuts the main door and drags a rack of leaflets in front of it. That ought to give them some time ...

It's just as before inside the building, the thick darkness driven back every so often by the flashes in the sky. The elderly lady is still at the ticket desk, but now she's holding her face with both hands, her eyes impossibly wide in fear, her mouth still distorted in a soundless howl of horror. Jake runs on with Hannah, past the exhibits and displays, past the glowing computer screens, each one showing a new picture now – Mum and Dad with James, all three of them smiling happily, no Jake and Hannah to be seen.

There's a sound of smashing glass as the main door is kicked in. Jake looks round just as a colossal flash floods the building with light. James is there behind them, his enormous shadow stretching long, groping hands across the floor in their direction. Then the darkness swoops down again.

'Ready or not, here I come!' James calls out, and laughs wildly.

Jake and Hannah are already running up the path to the stones.

EVIL VOICE

They hurry through the entrance to the circle, huge flashes splitting the sky above them, the ground trembling with the rumbles that follow. Jake's eyes are fixed on the inner ring and the dark bulk of the Heart Stone within it, and he speeds up, dragging Hannah along. He can hear her panting, his own breath coming in gasps, a solid, tight fist of pain beneath his breastbone.

He doesn't dare look back. He doesn't want to know how close behind James might be ... Nearly there, Jake thinks, as they reach the inner ring. Just a few metres more and Hannah can unmake her wish and they'll be safe.

Jake skids to a halt in the open space surrounding the Heart Stone, his trainers slipping on the grass, Hannah almost falling. Something doesn't feel right. He pulls Hannah close and looks around, trying to get his breathing under control, stop his heart pounding. It's as if they're being watched, Jake thinks, his skin tingling as it did when he first entered the circle. He can hear whispering too, a soft, evil voice hissing at them from every direction.

'*Jake ...*' the voice says, drawing his name out till it sounds like a dying breath. '*Hannah ... There's no hiding place in there. No hiding place at all ...*'

And then there's that wild laughter again, echoing round the stones.

'I don't like it, Jake,' says Hannah, her fingers digging into his arm.

'It's OK, Hannah,' Jake murmurs, a huge flash of lightning allowing him to scan the gaps between the inner stones. 'I can't see him anywhere ...'

Jake turns, starts to lead Hannah towards the Heart Stone. The next flash reveals it, barely a few metres in front of them. Darkness falls once more, swiftly followed by another flash from above. And now a tall, dark-cloaked figure is standing between them and the Heart Stone, its head lowered. But then the figure slowly looks up … and Jake sees that it's James.

A grinning James, who raises the cloak with both arms wide and laughs.

Jake is rigid with shock, and Hannah buries her face in his T-shirt.

'Boo,' James says quietly. 'Found you ... So it looks like I've won.'

'But ... how did you get here?' says Jake. 'You were behind us.'

'Oh, I'm full of tricks,' says James. 'Anyway, like the outfit? Pretty cool, isn't it? I told you there's plenty of power in this circle. But there are plenty of ghosts too, and I've learned a lot from one, a priest who used to have a special job here a long time ago. He's been helping me to see things a lot differently. You could even say I've incorporated him into my act. Maybe that's why I'm not the quiet, inoffensive little friend I used to be ...'

James strides forward and yanks Hannah from Jake's grasp as if she's a rag doll. She screams and struggles, but James soon puts a stop to that. He pulls her tight against him, a powerful arm across the throat silencing her.

'Leave her alone!' Jake yells, his voice almost breaking. 'Or I'll ...'

'Relax, Jake,' James says softly. 'I've just had a great idea. I could make you *my* imaginary friend once I've got rid of Hannah, and then it would be just us, two boys together with no sister taking all Mum and Dad's attention. How about it ... brother?' Suddenly James is holding a knife in his other hand, its leaf-shaped bronze blade glinting dully in a flash of lightning. James presses the point against Hannah's throat, his eyes on Jake. 'One little nick in Hannah's skin,' James murmurs, 'a few drops of blood and she's gone forever. And that's what you wanted, wasn't it, Jake? Hannah to die …'

Until then Jake has been trembling all over, but now he feels the shaking subside, his body go still as he stands there beneath James's gaze. Is it true? Had he wanted Hannah to die? He'd certainly hated her at times, but only because of what had happened, all the disruption and worry. And maybe once or twice he'd wished she'd never been born. But wanting her to die ...? Jake looks at his little sister, sees the fear in her eyes, but also a look that says she trusts him, and he knows that he loves her and wants her to live.

'No deal, *Mr* James,' says Jake. 'You've got me completely wrong.'

Hannah smiles at him, then opens her mouth, shows her small white teeth. She quickly flicks her eyes down at James's bare arm, then back up at Jake, and he gives her the tiniest of nods, understanding immediately what she's suggesting. But he also raises his hand slightly by his side, the fingers spread out, a warning to her to wait for the right moment, hoping James doesn't see.

Something is happening to distract James though. There's a rustling, a soft whispering like the sound of the wind sighing through a field of wheat.

James is looking at the gaps between the stones, and Jake does as well. Grey shapes drift through and gather in the space around the Heart Stone. Soon James and Jake and Hannah are surrounded by a ghostly host, the phantoms jostling for position, their spectral eyes bright stars

in a wavering mist.

'It seems we have an audience for the grand finale,' says James, smiling. 'Hardly surprising, really. This must be the most exciting thing to happen here for at least a couple of thousand years.' He turns his attention to Jake again. 'I'm disappointed in you too,' he says, taking the knife away from Hannah's throat and pointing it at Jake. 'You and your sister make a good pair. Neither of you can recognise a great opportunity when it's offered ...'

'Now, Hannah!' Jake yells, and Hannah instantly sinks her teeth into James's arm, biting deep with all her might, her eyes bulging with effort.

James looks down at her, utterly astonished, and he howls in pain.

'Why, you little …' he hisses, and throws her from him. She lands near the Heart Stone, rolls over a couple of times and scrambles to her feet.

'Quick, Hannah!' Jake almost screams at her. 'Unmake the wish …'

James is examining his arm, but looks up at Jake's words and realises what's happening. He moves forward, his face full of hate and violence, and Jake runs to meet him, seizing his knife arm, kicking out at him with his trainers, trying to give Hannah the time she needs. But James is far too strong, and grabs the front of Jake's T-shirt with his other hand, gathering a fistful of material and lifting him clean off the ground. James holds him in mid-air for a second, then slams him down on the Heart Stone and pins him there.

The impact drives the breath from Jake's body, but he still scrabbles at James's hand with his nails, and wriggles and kicks. It's no use. James bears down on him and Jake feels himself being crushed, his spine being ground into the rock beneath him, his ribs about to crack under the pressure.

Jake looks up at last, into the face of evil. James is grinning again. He tightens his grip on Jake's T-shirt and slowly raises his other arm on high. The leaf-shaped blade gleams in a colossal, sky-splitting flash of lightning.

'Game over, Jakey boy,' James murmurs, his black eyes glinting. He swings the knife down, the ghostly crowd letting out a sigh of pleasure.

Jake turns his head away, sees Hannah reaching towards the Heart Stone, screaming something he can't hear, her fingers a hair's breadth from the rock.

Suddenly, white light explodes in Jake's head, and he is falling, falling …

Epilogue

After a time, Jake realises his eyes are closed and he opens them. He sees three faces above him, two large and one small, each wearing an expression of concern. Mum, Dad and Hannah, an enormous blue sky behind them.

'He's coming round,' says Mum, and she and Dad help him sit up. 'Are you OK, love?' says Mum. 'You went down like you'd been pole-axed.'

'I'm fine, Mum,' says Jake, and gets to his feet, Mum and Dad holding on to him. Jake checks himself over. Red T-shirt, blue jeans, white trainers. Then he checks the surroundings. The four of them are near the Heart Stone, and the sky is full of warm sunshine, exactly the way it was when they arrived, except that the big, fluffy white cloud has vanished. But James has gone too, and so have the ghosts. Finally Jake checks his sister. He notices a faint red mark on the pale skin of her neck, but otherwise she seems perfectly all right. Their eyes meet and she smiles. 'I just felt a bit ... odd,' Jake says.

'You've probably had too much sun,' says Dad. 'It's very hot.'

'Oh, Jake,' Mum says suddenly, guilt and anguish in her voice. She puts a cool hand on his forehead to feel whether he's got a temperature. 'You should be wearing a hat on a day like this, and suncream, like Hannah. I'm so sorry, love. We don't seem to have been taking proper care of you recently ...'

'Don't worry about it, Mum,' says Jake. 'It wasn't your fault.'

'You're sure you feel OK?' says Mum. 'Not dizzy, or sick, or …'

'No, Mum, honest,' says Jake. 'Really, I've never felt better.'

'That's good,' Mum says. 'I'll keep an eye on you, just the same.' She looks deep into his eyes. Then she smiles and kisses his cheek.

'I think you might be hungry, as well,' says Dad. 'I know I am. In fact, I'm absolutely starving. And we've had our dose of history for today. Those in favour of supper at that pizza place we saw yesterday, follow me.'

So the family leaves the inner ring, Mum with her arm around Jake's shoulders, Dad in front with Hannah, both of them looking back at Jake from time to time, concern still in their eyes. They reach the Visitor Centre, Jake feeling nervous as they enter, afraid of what he might see. But everything is as it should be – families milling around the exhibits, the elderly lady at the ticket desk back to normal. She cheerily bids them goodbye as they go out.

The car park is busy again. Dad unlocks

the people carrier, and they get into their familiar seats. Dad starts the engine, and they drive off, leaving the stones behind. Jake looks at the grove of trees. A gust of wind swishes through the branches and across a picnic table, angrily flicking open the pages of a comic somebody has left there. Jake doesn't ask Dad to stop.

'You two OK in the back?' Dad says, his eyes on Jake and Hannah in the rear-view mirror. Mum turns round as well. 'Or should I say you three?'

'There's only two of us,' Hannah says firmly. Then she peeks at Jake across the small space between them. 'Just me … and my horrible brother.'

But she grins as she says it. Jake reaches over and tickles her, and she squeals and squirms away from him, and he laughs. Mum and Dad glance at each other, and raise their eyebrows in surprise. Then they laugh too.

Jake is still smiling as they turn on to the main road and head for the pizza place, the tyres thrumming smoothly on the tarmac beneath him.

He's sure the rest of the day is going to be a lot of fun, after all.

CAPTAIN FACT's
HUMAN BODY ADVENTURE

WHENEVER DISASTER STRIKES, MILD-MANNERED WEATHERMAN CLIFF THORNHILL AND HIS DOG PUDDLES ARE TRANSFORMED INTO . . . **CAPTAIN FACT AND KNOWLEDGE!**

MINIATURISED TO THE SIZE OF A MOLECULE, OUR HEROES ARE INJECTED INTO A REAL LIVE HUMAN BODY. HERE THEY MUST INVESTIGATE INNARDS AND EXAMINE EARWAX TO HUNT DOWN A VICIOUS VIRUS THAT'S CAUSING A TRANSGLOBAL OUTBREAK OF BOTTOM BOILS! WITH A MEDICAL ENCYCLOPAEDIA OF FACTS AT THEIR FINGERTIPS, CAN CAPTAIN FACT AND KNOWLEDGE SAVE THE DAY?

FIND OUT EVERYTHING YOU EVER WANTED TO KNOW ABOUT YOUR OWN INSIDES IN THEIR **FACT-TASTIC** HUMAN BODY ADVENTURE!